The bearer of this scroll, namely,

is a master in the
Order of the Kai

Lone Wolf 6

The Kingdoms of Terror

THE AUTHOR AND THE ILLUSTRATOR

JOE DEVER was born in 1956 at Woodford Bridge in Essex. When he first left college, he became a full-time musician with a large London recording studio. Then on a business trip to Los Angeles in 1977, he discovered a role-playing game called 'Dungeons and Dragons' and was instantly hooked. In 1982 he won the Advanced Dungeons and Dragons Championship in America, where he was the only British competitor. He has since appeared on national TV, radio and in the papers in connection with his hobby.

The Lone Wolf adventures are the culmination of many years of developing the world of Magnamund, and Joe looks forward to revealing more of the wonders of the Lastlands in future books.

Born in 1952, GARY CHALK grew up in rural Hertfordshire. Through an interest in history, he began playing wargames at the age of fifteen – a hobby he still enjoys today. When he first graduated from college with a BA in design, Gary spent three years training in a studio before becoming a teacher in art and design.

He was working as a children's book illustrator when he became involved in adventure gaming, an interest which eventually led to the creation of several successful games including 'Cry Havoc', 'Starship Captain' and 'Battlecars' (co-designed with Ian Livingstone). He is perhaps best known for his work on the very successful 'Talisman' game.

LONE WOLF 6

The Kingdoms of Terror

Joe Dever

Illustrated by Gary Chalk
Cover by Brian Salmon

Beaver Books

A Beaver Book
Published by Arrow Books Limited
62–65 Chandos Place, London WC2N 4NW

An imprint of Century Hutchinson Ltd

London Melbourne Sydney Auckland
Johannesburg and agencies throughout the world

First published 1985
Reprinted 1986 and 1988

Set in Linoterm Souvenir Light
by JH Graphics Ltd, Reading, Berks

Printed and bound in Great Britain
by Anchor Brendon Ltd,
Tiptree, Essex

ISBN 0 09 944460 7

To Philippa and Alison

ACTION CHART

MAGNAKAI DISCIPLINES   NOTES

1	
2	
3	

MAGNAKAI LORE - CIRCLE   BONUSES

	CS	EP		CS	EP
CIRCLE OF FIRE	+1	+2	**CIRCLE OF SOLARIS**	+1	+3
CIRCLE OF LIGHT	0	+3	**CIRCLE OF THE SPIRIT**	+3	+3

BACKPACK (max. 8 articles)

	MEALS
1	
2	
3	— 3 EP if no Meal available when instructed to eat.
4	**BELT POUCH** Containing Gold Crowns (50 maximum)
5	
6	
7	
8	

Can be discarded when not in combat.

EP = ENDURANCE POINTS   CS = COMBAT SKILL

COMBAT SKILL	ENDURANCE POINTS
	Can never go above initial score 0 = dead

COMBAT RECORD

ENDURANCE POINTS   **ENDURANCE POINTS**

LONE WOLF	COMBAT RATIO	ENEMY
LONE WOLF	COMBAT RATIO	ENEMY
LONE WOLF	COMBAT RATIO	ENEMY
LONE WOLF	COMBAT RATIO	ENEMY
LONE WOLF	COMBAT RATIO	ENEMY

MAGNAKAI RANK

SPECIAL ITEMS LIST

DESCRIPTION	KNOWN EFFECTS

WEAPONS LIST

WEAPONS (maximum 2 Weapons)

1	
2	

If holding Weapon and appropriate **Weaponmastery** in combat +2 CS. If combat entered carrying no Weapon —4 CS.

WEAPONMASTERY CHECKLIST

DAGGER		SPEAR	
MACE		SHORT SWORD	
WARHAMMER		BOW	
AXE		SWORD	
QUARTERSTAFF		BROADSWORD	

QUIVER & ARROWS

Quiver	No. of arrows carried
YES/NO	

THE STORY SO FAR . . .

You are Kai Master Lone Wolf – last of the Kai Lords of Sommerlund and the sole survivor of a massacre that destroyed your warrior kinsmen during a bitter war with your age-old enemies, the Darklords of Helgedad.

Three years have passed since your triumph over the Darklord Haakon at the Tomb of the Majhan and, for the northern realm of Sommerlund, these have been three years of peace and prosperity. Since Haakon's defeat, the power of the Darklords has waned. Rumours abound that a civil war rages in Helgedad, as the lesser Darklords fight for power and dominion over the city. However, it is a widely held belief in Sommerlund that your discovery of the lost Sommlending treasure, *The Book of the Magnakai*, is the real reason for their power struggle.

The Book of the Magnakai is legendary in Sommerlund. With the wisdom of the Magnakai, Sun Eagle, the first Kai Grand Master, instilled the disciplines into the warriors of Sommerlund that were to protect your land from devastation at the hands of the Darklords. *The Book of the Magnakai* was lost hundreds of years ago, but its wisdom was kept alive, handed down through generations of Kai so that they too could share the strength to resist their eternal enemies.

11

When you discovered *The Book of the Magnakai*, you gave a solemn pledge to restore the Kai to their former glory and so ensure the security of your land in the years to come. You returned to your homeland and, in the seclusion of your monastery in the hills, set about the study of the Magnakai disciplines. It was an exacting task – a trial of physical strength and mental fortitude. The seasons came and went but you were unaware of the passage of time, lost in your quest for the knowledge and the skills of your warrior kin. Three years of determined study pass, revealing the secrets of three of the Magnakai disciplines. However, the others cannot be learnt by study alone and, in order to fulfil your pledge to restore the Kai, you must complete the quest first made by Sun Eagle over a thousand years ago. When he had finally completed his quest, he recorded all his experiences in *The Book of the Magnakai*; but the script has faded with the passing years and now few words remain to guide you.

'Seek and find the Lorestone of Varetta for this alone holds the power and the wisdom . . .' are the few words you can still decipher of the Grand Master's chronicle.

Although the verse is brief you are not without hope, for you recognize the name Varetta. It is one of the oldest cities of Magnamund, lying in the Stornlands beyond the Maakengorge, far to the south of Sommerlund. You realize that you must set out upon the quest without delay, for the war in Helgedad will not last indefinitely and the Darklords swore long ago to conquer your country and destroy your people. As soon as their civil strife is resolved, the victorious lords of evil will turn on Sommerlund and summon the creatures of the Dark Realm to thwart your quest. You must therefore act quickly and with secrecy, for your life and the future of Sommerlund depends on your success.

And so, guided by the words of your ancient mentor and with the shadow of the Darklords ever present, you set out on the quest for the Lorestone of Varetta, unaware of the wonders and the horrors that await you in the Stornlands.

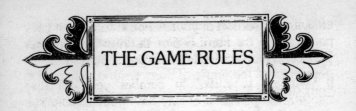

THE GAME RULES

You keep a record of your adventure on the *Action Chart* that you will find in the front of this book. For further adventuring you can copy out the chart yourself or get it photocopied.

During your training as a Kai Master you have developed fighting prowess – COMBAT SKILL and physical stamina – ENDURANCE. Before you set off on your adventure you need to measure how effective your training has been. To do this take a pencil and, with your eyes closed, point with the blunt end of it on to the *Random Number Table* on the last page of this book. If you pick *0* it counts as zero.

The first number that you pick from the *Random Number Table* in this way represents your COMBAT SKILL. Add 10 to the number you picked and write the total in the COMBAT SKILL section of your *Action Chart.* (ie, if your pencil fell on the number 4 in the *Random Number Table* you would write in a COMBAT SKILL of 14.) When you fight, your COMBAT SKILL will be pitted against that of your enemy. A high score in this section is therefore very desirable.

The second number that you pick from the *Random Number Table* represents your powers of ENDURANCE. Add 20 to this number and write the total in the

ENDURANCE section of your *Action Chart*. (ie, if your pencil fell on the number 6 on the *Random Number Table* you would have 26 ENDURANCE points.)

If you are wounded in combat you will lose ENDURANCE points. If at any time your ENDURANCE points fall to zero, you are dead and the adventure is over. Lost ENDURANCE points can be regained during the course of the adventure, but your number of ENDURANCE points can never rise above the number you started with.

If you have successfully completed any of the previous adventures in the Lone Wolf series, Books 1—5, you can carry your current scores of Combat Skill and Endurance Points over to the 'Magnakai' series. You may also carry over any Weapons and Special Items you have in your possession at the end of your last adventure, and these should be entered on your new Action Chart (you are still limited to two Weapons and eight Backpack Items).

MAGNAKAI DISCIPLINES

During your training as a Kai Lord, and in the course of the adventures that led to the discovery of *The Book of the Magnakai*, you have mastered all ten of the basic warrior skills known as the Kai Disciplines.

After studying *The Book of the Magnakai*, *you* have also reached the rank of Kai Master Superior, which means that you have learnt *three* of the

Magnakai Disciplines listed below. It is up to you to choose which three skills these are. As all of the Magnakai Disciplines will be of use to you at some point on your adventure, pick your three with care. The correct use of a Magnakai Discipline at the right time can save your life.

The Magnakai skills are divided into groups, each of which is governed by a separate school of training. These groups are called 'Lore-circles'. By mastering all of the Magnakai Disciplines in a particular Lore-circle, you can gain an increase in your COMBAT SKILL and ENDURANCE points score. (See the section 'Lore-circles of the Magnakai' for details of these bonuses.)

When you have chosen your three Magnakai Disciplines, enter them in the Magnakai Disciplines section of your *Action Chart*.

Weaponmastery
This Magnakai Discipline enables a Kai Master to become proficient in the use of all types of weapon. When you enter combat with a weapon you have mastered, you add 3 points to your COMBAT SKILL. The rank of Kai Master Superior, with which you begin the Magnakai series, means you are skilled in *three* of the weapons in the list below.

DAGGER

16

SPEAR

MACE

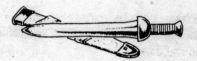

SHORT SWORD

WARHAMMER

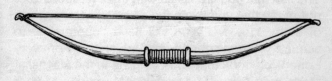

BOW

AXE

SWORD

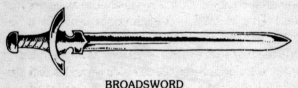

QUARTERSTAFF

BROADSWORD

The fact that you are skilled with three weapons does not mean that you begin the adventure carrying any of them. However, you will have opportunities to acquire weapons during your adventure. For every Lone Wolf book that you complete in the Magnakai series, you may add an additional weapon to your list.

If you choose this skill, write 'Weaponmastery: + 3 COMBAT SKILL points' on your *Action Chart*, and tick your chosen weapons on the weapons list that appears on page 10. You cannot carry more than two weapons.

Animal Control

This Magnakai Discipline enables a Kai Master to communicate with most animals and to determine their purpose and intentions. It also enables a Kai Master to fight from the saddle with great advantage.

If you choose this skill, write 'Animal Control' on your *Action Chart*.

Curing

The possessor of this skill can restore 1 lost ENDURANCE point to his total for every numbered section of the book through which he passes, provided he is not involved in combat. (This can only be done after his ENDURANCE has fallen below its original level.) This Magnakai Discipline also enables a Kai Master to cure disease, blindness and any combat wounds sustained by others, as well as himself. Using the knowledge mastery of this skill provides will also allow a Kai Master to identify the properties of any herbs, roots and potions that may be encountered during the adventure.

If you choose this skill, write 'Curing: + 1 ENDURANCE point for each section without combat' on your *Action Chart*.

Invisibility

This Magnakai skill allows a Kai Master to blend in

with his surroundings, even in the most exposed terrain. It will enable him to mask his body heat and scent, and to adopt the dialect and mannerisms of any town or city that he visits.

If you choose this skill, write 'Invisibility' on your *Action Chart*.

Huntmastery
This skill ensures that a Kai Master will never starve in the wild; he will always be able to hunt for food, even in areas of wasteland and desert. It also enables a Kai Master to move with great speed and dexterity and will allow him to ignore any extra loss of COMBAT SKILL points due to a surprise attack or ambush.

If you choose this skill, write 'Huntmastery' on your *Action Chart*.

Pathsmanship
In addition to the basic skill of being able to recognize the correct path in unknown territory, the Magnakai skill of Pathsmanship will enable a Kai Master to read foreign languages, decipher symbols, read footprints and tracks (even if they have been disturbed), and detect the presence of most traps. It also grants him the gift of always knowing intuitively the position of north.

If you choose this skill, write 'Pathsmanship' on your *Action Chart*.

Psi-surge
This psychic skill enables a Kai Master to attack an enemy using the force of his mind. It can be used as

well as normal combat weapons and adds 4 extra points to your COMBAT SKILL.

It is a powerful Discipline, but it is also a costly one. For every round of combat in which you use Psi-surge, you must deduct 2 ENDURANCE points. A weaker form of Psi-surge called Mindblast can be used against an enemy without losing any ENDURANCE points, but it will add only 2 extra points to your COMBAT SKILL. Psi-surge cannot be used if your ENDURANCE falls to 6 points or below, and not all of the creatures encountered on your adventure will be affected by it; you will be told if a creature is immune.

If you choose this skill, write 'Psi-surge: +4 COMBAT SKILL points but −2 ENDURANCE points per round' and 'Mindblast: +2 COMBAT SKILL points' on your *Action Chart*.

Psi-screen

Many of the hostile creatures that inhabit Magnamund have the ability to attack you using their Mindforce. The Magnakai Discipline of Psi-screen prevents you from losing any ENDURANCE points when subjected to this form of attack and greatly increases your defence against supernatural illusions and hypnosis.

If you choose this skill, write 'Psi-screen: no points lost when attacked by Mindforce' on your *Action Chart*.

Nexus

Mastery of this Magnakai skill will enable you to withstand extremes of heat and cold without losing

ENDURANCE points, and to move items by your powers of concentration alone.

If you choose this skill, write 'Nexus' on your *Action Chart*.

Divination

This skill may warn a Kai Master of imminent or unseen danger, or enable him to detect an invisible or hidden enemy. It may also reveal the true purpose or intent of a stranger or strange object encountered in your adventure. Divination may enable you to communicate telepathically with another person and to sense if a creature possesses psychic abilities.

If you choose this skill, write 'Divination' on your *Action Chart*.

If you successfully complete the mission as set in Book 6 of the Lone Wolf series, you may add a further Magnakai Discipline of your choice to your *Action Chart* in Book 7. This additional skill, together with your three other Magnakai skills and any Special Items that you have found and been able to keep during your adventures may then be used in the next adventure in the Lone Wolf Magnakai series, which is called *Castle Death*.

EQUIPMENT

Before leaving Sommerlund on your quest for the Lorestone of Varetta, you equip yourself with a map of the Stornlands (see front inside cover) and a pouch of gold. To find out how much gold is in the pouch,

22

pick a number from the *Random Number Table*. Add 10 to the number you have picked. The total equals the number of Gold Crowns inside the pouch and you should now enter this number in the 'Gold Crowns' section of your *Action Chart*. If you have successfully completed books 1–5 of the Lone Wolf adventures in the earlier series, you may add this sum to the total of any Crowns you already possess. You can only carry a maximum of fifty Crowns, but any over this number can be left in safe keeping at your Kai monastery.

You can take five items from the list below, again adding to these, if necessary, any you may already possess. However, remember you can only carry two weapons and eight Backpack Items, maximum.

SWORD (Weapons)

POTION OF LAUMSPUR (Backpack Items) This potion restores 4 ENDURANCE points to your total when swallowed after combat. There is enough for only one dose.

WARHAMMER (Weapons)

BOW (Weapons)

QUIVER (Special Items) This contains six arrows. Tick them off as they are used.

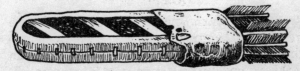

4 SPECIAL RATIONS (Meals) Each of these counts as one Meal, and each takes up one space in your Backpack.

QUARTERSTAFF (Weapons)
PADDED LEATHER WAISTCOAT (Special Item) This adds 2 ENDURANCE points to your total.

ROPE (Backpack Items)

DAGGER (Weapons)
TINDERBOX (Backpack Items)

AXE (Weapons)

List the five items that you choose on your *Action Chart*, under the heading given in brackets, and make a note of any effect it may have on your ENDURANCE points or COMBAT SKILL.

How to carry equipment

Now that you have your equipment, the following list shows you how it is carried. You do not need to make notes but you should refer back to this list in the course of your adventure.

SWORD – carried in the hand.
POTION OF LAUMSPUR – carried in the Backpack.
WARHAMMER – carried in the hand.
BOW – carried in the hand.
QUIVER – slung over your shoulder.
SPECIAL RATIONS – carried in the Backpack.
QUARTERSTAFF – carried in the hand.
PADDED LEATHER WAISTCOAT – worn on the body.
ROPE – carried in the Backpack.
DAGGER – carried in the hand.
TINDERBOX carried in the Backpack.
AXE – carried in the hand

How much can you carry?

Weapons
The maximum number of weapons that you may carry is *two*.

Backpack Items
These must be stored in your Backpack. Because space is limited, you may keep a maximum of only eight articles, including Meals, in your Backpack at any one time.

Special Items
Special Items are not carried in the Backpack. When you discover a Special Item, you will be told how to carry it.

Gold Crowns
These are always carried in the Belt Pouch. It will hold a maximum of fifty Crowns.

Food
Food is carried in your Backpack. Each Meal counts as one item.

Any item that may be of use and can be picked up on your adventure and entered on your *Action Chart* is given initial capitals (eg Gold Dagger, Magic Pendant) in the text. Unless you are told it is a Special Item, carry it in your Backpack.

How to use your equipment

Weapons
Weapons aid you in combat. If you have the Magnakai Discipline of Weaponmastery and a correct weapon, it adds 3 points to your COMBAT SKILL. If you enter a combat with no weapons, deduct 4 points from your COMBAT SKILL and fight with your bare hands. If you find a weapon during the adventure, you may pick it up and use it. (Remember that you can only carry *two* weapons at once.)

Bow and Arrows
During your adventure there will be opportunities to use a bow and arrow. If you equip yourself with this weapon, and you possess at least one arrow, you

may use it when the text of a particular section allows you to do so. The bow is a useful weapon, for it enables you to hit an enemy at a distance. However, a bow cannot be used in hand-to-hand combat, therefore it is strongly recommended that you also equip yourself with a close combat weapon, like a sword or mace.

In order to use a bow you must possess a quiver and at least one arrow. Each time the bow is used, erase an arrow from your *Action Chart*. A bow cannot, of course, be used if you exhaust your supply of arrows, but the opportunity may arise during your adventure for you to replenish your stock of arrows.

If you have the Magnakai Discipline of Weapon-mastery with a bow, you may add 3 to any number that you choose from the *Random Number Table*, when using the bow. If you enter combat armed only with a bow, you must deduct 4 points from your COMBAT SKILL and fight with your bare hands.

Backpack Items
During your travels you will discover various useful items which you may wish to keep. (Remember you can only carry a maximum of eight items in your Backpack at any time.) You may exchange or discard them at any point when you are not involved in combat.

Special Items
Special Items are not carried in the Backpack. When you discover a Special Item, you will be told how to carry it. If you have successfully completed previous Lone Wolf books, you may already possess Special Items.

Gold Crowns

The currency of Sommerlund and the Stornlands is the Crown, which is a small gold coin. Whenever you kill an enemy and search the body, you may take any Gold Crowns that you find and put them in your Belt Pouch. (Remember the pouch can carry a maximum of fifty Gold Crowns.)

Food

You will need to eat regularly during your adventure. If you do not have any food when you are instructed to eat a Meal, you will lose 3 ENDURANCE POINTS. If you have chosen the Magnakai Discipline of HUNT-MASTERY as one of your skills, you will not need to tick off a Meal when instructed to eat.

Potion of Laumspur

This is a healing potion that can restore 4 ENDURANCE points to your total when swallowed after combat. There is enough for one dose only. If you discover any other potion during the adventure, you will be informed of its effect. All potions are Backpack Items.

RULES FOR COMBAT

There will be occasions during your adventure when you have to fight an enemy. The enemy's COMBAT SKILL and ENDURANCE points are given in the text. Lone Wolf's aim in the combat is to kill the enemy by reducing his ENDURANCE points to zero while losing as few ENDURANCE points as possible himself.

28

At the start of a combat, enter Lone Wolf's and the enemy's ENDURANCE points in the appropriate boxes on the Combat Record section of your *Action Chart*.

The sequence for combat is as follows:

1. Add any extra points gained through your Magnakai Disciplines and Special Items to your current COMBAT SKILL total.

2. Subtract the COMBAT SKILL of your enemy from this total. The result is your *Combat Ratio*. Enter it on the *Action Chart*.

Example

Lone Wolf (COMBAT SKILL 15) is attacked by a Nightstalker (COMBAT SKILL 22). He is not given the opportunity to evade combat, but must stand and fight as the creature leaps on him. Lone Wolf has the Magnakai Discipline of Psi-surge to which the Nightstalker is not immune, so Lone Wolf adds 4 points to his COMBAT SKILL, giving a total COMBAT SKILL of 19.

He subtracts the Nightstalker's COMBAT SKILL from his own, giving a *Combat Ratio* of −3. (19 − 22 = −3). −3 is noted on the *Action Chart* as the *Combat Ratio*.

3. When you have your *Combat Ratio*, pick a number from the *Random Number Table*.

4. Turn to the *Combat Results Table* on the inside back cover of the book. Along the top of the chart are shown the *Combat Ratio* numbers. Find the number that is the same as your *Combat Ratio* and cross-reference it with the random number

that you have picked (the random numbers appear on the side of the chart). You now have the number of ENDURANCE points lost by both Lone Wolf and his enemy in this round of combat. (*E* represents points lost by the enemy; *LW* represents points lost by Lone Wolf.)

Example

The *Combat Ratio* between Lone Wolf and the Nightstalker has been established as −3. If the number taken from the *Random Number Table* is a 6, then the result of the first round of combat is:

Lone Wolf loses 3 ENDURANCE points (plus an additional 2 points for using Psi-surge)
Nightstalker loses 6 ENDURANCE points

5. On the *Action Chart*, mark the changes in ENDURANCE points to the participants in the combat.

6. Unless otherwise instructed, or unless you have an option to evade, the next round of combat now starts.

7. Repeat the sequence from Stage 3.

This process of combat continues until the ENDURANCE points of either the enemy or Lone Wolf are reduced to zero, at which point the one with the zero score is declared dead. If Lone Wolf is dead, the adventure is over. If the enemy is dead, Lone Wolf proceeds but with his ENDURANCE points reduced.

A summary of Combat Rules appears on the page after the *Random Number Table.*

Evasion of combat

During your adventure you may be given the chance to evade combat. If you have already engaged in a round of combat and decide to evade, calculate the combat for that round in the usual manner. All points lost by the enemy as a result of that round are ignored, and you make your escape. Only Lone Wolf may lose ENDURANCE points during that round, but then that is the risk of running away! You may only evade if the text of the particular section allows you to do so.

LEVELS OF MAGNAKAI TRAINING

The following table is a guide to the rank and titles that are achieved by Kai Masters at each stage of their training. As you successfully complete each adventure in the Lone Wolf Magnakai series, you will gain an additional Magnakai Discipline and progress towards the ultimate distinction of a Kai Warrior – Kai Grand Mastership.

No. of Magnakai Disciplines mastered by Kai Master	Magnakai Rank
1	Kai Master
2	Kai Master Senior
3	Kai Master Superior – *You begin the Lone Wolf Magnakai adventures with this level of training.*
4	*Primate*
5	*Tutelary*
6	*Principalin*
7	*Mentora*
8	*Scion-kai*
9	*Archmaster*
10	*Kai Grand Master*

LORE-CIRCLES OF THE MAGNAKAI

In the years before their massacre, the Kai Masters of Sommerlund devoted themselves to the study of the Magnakai. These skills were divided into four schools of training called 'Lore-circles'. By mastering all of the Magnakai Disciplines of a Lore-circle, the Kai Masters developed their fighting prowess (COMBAT SKILL), and their physical and mental stamina (ENDURANCE) to a level far higher than any mortal warrior could otherwise attain.

Listed below are the four Lore-circles of the Magnakai and the skills that must be mastered in order to complete them.

Title of Magnakai Lore-circle	Magnakai Disciplines needed to complete the Lore-circle
CIRCLE OF FIRE	Weaponmastery & Huntmastery
CIRCLE OF LIGHT	Animal control & Curing
CIRCLE OF SOLARIS	Invisiblity, Huntmastery & Pathsmanship
CIRCLE OF THE SPIRIT	Psi-surge, Psi-shield, Nexus & Divination

By completing a Lore-circle, you may add to your COMBAT SKILL and ENDURANCE the extra bonus points that are shown below.

Lore circle bonuses

	COMBAT SKILL	ENDURANCE
CIRCLE OF FIRE	+1	+2
CIRCLE OF LIGHT	0	+3
CIRCLE OF SOLARIS	+1	+3
CIRCLE OF THE SPIRIT	+3	+3

All bonus points that you acquire by completing a Lore-circle are additions to your basic COMBAT SKILL and ENDURANCE scores.

IMPROVED DISCIPLINES

As you rise through the higher levels of Magnakai training you will find that each of your skills will steadily improve. For example, if you possess the discipline of Divination when you reach the Magnakai rank of Scion-kai, you will be able to 'Spirit Walk' and leave your body in a state of suspended animation as you explore your immediate surroundings unhindered by physical limitations.

The nature of these additional improvements and how they affect your Magnakai Disciplines will be noted in the 'Improved Disciplines' section of future Lone Wolf books.

MAGNAKAI WISDOM

Your quest for the Lorestone of Varetta will be fraught with danger, for the lands that border upon the River Storn are wild and turbulent nations, constantly warring with one another. Use the map at the front of the book to help you during your adventure and make notes as you progress through the story, for they will be of great help in this and future adventures.

Many things that you find will help you during your adventure. Some Special Items will be of use in future Lone Wolf adventures and others may be red herrings of no real use at all, so be selective in what you decide to keep.

Choose your three Magnakai Disciplines with care, for a wise choice can enable any player to complete the quest no matter how weak his initial COMBAT SKILL and ENDURANCE points scores. Successful completion of previous Lone Wolf adventures, although an advantage, is not essential for the completion of this Magnakai adventure.

May the spirit of Sun Eagle guide you on the path of the Magnakai.

Good Luck!

1

The courtyard of the Kai monastery is strangely silent the morning you begin the quest. A blanket of frost sparkles on the battlements and the air is crisp and clear as you guide your horse down the steep hill track that disappears into the Fryelund forest. It is only a little later when you look back to see the tall grey towers of your stronghold silhouetted against the sky. You bid a silent farewell before entering the densely packed trees. You do not look back again.

The long ride south is not without incident. On Raider's Road, the highway between the capital and the province of Ruanon, you are confronted by a ragged outlaw band. They demand gold but instead receive a harsh lesson in the powers of a Kai Master. You fight them and they flee in confusion, leaving three of their number dead on the highway. After this encounter, you are given a wide berth by all the other unsavoury characters of this bleak and desolate region.

In Ruanon, you are greeted with a hero's welcome by the lord of the land, Baron Vanalund. He and his people will never forget the debt they owe you, for it was your courage that once saved them from destruction at the hands of an evil renegade warlord. You are made so welcome by the Ruanese that your quest is in danger of being forgotten in the endless round of banquets and celebrations held in your honour. However, you cannot neglect your duty and the time soon comes for you to leave the mining town and venture south once more.

Long ago, the highway from Ruanon to Quarlen was torn in two by a terrible earthquake that scarred the land for hundreds of miles. This deep crevasse became known as the Maakengorge – the chasm of doom – for its fathomless depths are cursed with a dreadful legacy. It was here, during the Age of the Black Moon, that King Ulnar killed the mightiest of the Darklords – Lord Vashna, whose body, along with the bodies of all his followers, was cast down into its bottomless reach. The legends say that his death cry will echo through the gorge until he rises again to wreak his vengeance on Sommerlund and the House of Ulnar.

You are eager to avoid the chasm of doom and the long detour to the free city-state of Casiorn is a far better prospect than a visit to the ghost-city of Maaken. Gradually, the fertile plain of southern Ruanon gives way to the sparse vegetation on the borders of the Dry Main. There, like a jewel rising out of the desert, lies the city-state of Casiorn. Your stay in the City of Merchants is a brief but profitable one; a piece of luck helped by your Kai skills, gives a profitable win at the gambling house of the Silver Sage. With the gold you win you replenish your supplies and purchase a fresh mount for your ride to Quarlen.

A week later, you arrive safely at the outskirts of Quarlen and, in the evening twilight, find yourself gazing upon the fortified wall that surrounds this river town. To reach Varetta you must cross the river – and only here, at Quarlen, is there a bridge that spans the fast-flowing waters of the Quarl. The highway divides as it approaches the town wall, for there are two gates that provide access to its east side.

If you wish to approach the north gate, turn to **137**.

If you wish to approach the south gate, turn to **225**.

If you have the Magnakai Discipline of Pathsmanship, turn to **308**.

2

Several of the smaller stoppered glass jars contain potions that could be of use to you on your quest. As you peer along the shelves you look carefully at their labels:

Potion of Laumspur (restores 4 ENDURANCE points per dose) – 5 Gold Crowns

Potion of Gallowbrush (induces sleep for 1—2 hours per dose) – 2 Gold Crowns

Rendalim's Elixir (restores 6 ENDURANCE points per dose) – 7 Gold Crowns

Potion of Alether (increases COMBAT SKILL by 2 for the duration of one combat) – 4 Gold Crowns

Graveweed Concentrate (causes death if swallowed) – 4 Gold Crowns

You may purchase any of the above potions, all of which are Backpack Items.

If you wish to look at some of the other shops in this street, turn to **152**.

If you decide to wait for the captain to be served, turn to **231**.

3

At the top of the hill the track comes to an abrupt end at a tall circle of stones. A bundle of firewood is stacked in the centre of the circle and a Torch, wrapped in oilcloth, lies nearby. You recognize this as a signal beacon, for they are very common in Sommerlund, especially along the border with the Durncrag mountains. If you wish you may take the Torch before heading back along the track.

Turn to **330**.

4

As you move the strands aside they suddenly begin to writhe and twist like a seething mass of snakes, coiling round your weapon and turning it back towards your hand. You release your grip and fall back in horror as your weapon is consumed in their corrosive grasp.

You turn and run back towards the junction, your stomach churning as you realize how close you came to a grisly death. Erase your lost weapon from your *Action Chart* before choosing which channel to take.

If you wish to go straight ahead, turn to **339**.
If you wish to take the channel to your left, turn to **269**.

5

A shrill cockcrow heralds the break of day. By the time you have dressed and gathered together your equipment, Cyrilus is waiting for you in the courtyard below.

'A glorious day,' he says cheerfully, pointing up at the cloudless sky with his slender oaken staff. 'We'll have no difficulty reaching the Halfway Inn by nightfall.'

You bid farewell to the innkeeper and his son and urge your horses out on to the narrow street that leads to the west gatehouse. By mid-morning you are riding across gentle hills crested with yellow-leaved trees. The hilltops are shrouded with mist but occasional rays of sunshine break through to lighten the lush green fields below. Time passes swiftly as Cyrilus recounts the histories and legends of the area. You learn that the rich and fertile kingdoms bordering the River Storn have a wild and turbulent past, swept by wars, divided by empires, split by national rivalries and the ambitions of petty princes who prey upon one another and the rest of the populace. Lyris is embroiled in war with Magador, Delden with Salony and Salony with Slovia. Battles are fought, lives are lost and the land is pillaged with grim regularity – only the mercenaries and the crows seem to prosper from the continual conflicts.

It is mid-afternoon when you catch sight of a small village on the road ahead. There are many wagons parked at the side of the highway and a crowd has gathered in a field nearby. As you ride past, you notice a large placard nailed to one of the wagons:

ARCHERY TOURNAMENT
ENTRANCE FEE: 2 GOLD CROWNS
FIRST PRIZE: THE SILVER BOW OF DUADON

If you wish to enter the tournament, turn to **141**.
If you do not wish to or cannot afford to enter, continue on your way and turn to **210**.

'Calm yourselves, my brothers. It is he – it is the Kai Lord.'

Slowly, as the startled old men regain their composure, their shocked expressions change to ones of awe and reverence.

'I am Gwynian,' says their leader. 'We have been expecting your arrival.' He points to the charts that cover the table, and to a massive telescope that is fixed to a platform in the domed ceiling.

'The stars divine the shape of things to come – they are our advisors. We know of your quest for the Lorestone. We know that it is the true quest and we pledge our help, but there are many of our brethren who fear its power. They choose to ignore the wisdom of the stars and they have pledged themselves to a foolish and dangerous vow to keep hidden the location of the Lorestone and to kill all who seek it, for fear they would use it for their own ends.'

Suddenly, his words are cut short by the beating of fists against the observatory door: your horse has been discovered.

'Give him to us!' shouts a chorus of angry voices.

'Quickly, we must leave,' says Gwynian, and he ushers you into a smaller room. A hidden catch is pulled and a secret panel opens to reveal a passage. As you follow the sage and his companions into the darkness, you hear the door to the observatory splinter and break.

Turn to **158**.

7

You sense tension and imminent danger all around you. The quiet serenity of this little hamlet is deceptive – beneath it is hidden a deadly threat to your safety. Instinctively, you unsheathe your weapon and prepare to defend yourself in case of a sudden ambush.

Turn to **258**.

8

Chanda gasps and shudders as your final blow robs him of all his strength. He tries to curse you but the words stick in his throat. As he fights to speak he stumbles and falls dead at your feet.

You turn him over with the toe of your boot and make a quick but thorough search of his body. You discover a pouch containing 10 Gold Crowns, a Potion of Laumspur (enough to restore 3 ENDURANCE points) and a Map of Varetta. (Mark this as a Special Item, which is carried in your Backpack.) You may take any of these items if you wish and leave this eerie shop.

Turn to **16**.

9

The guards exchange glances and nod their heads in agreement. 'Ten Gold Crowns will make you a welcome guest in our town, stranger,' whispers the shorter of the two men, holding out his gauntleted hand in expectation.

If you wish to pay the bribe, turn to **332**.

(contd over)

If you do not wish to pay so large a sum and wish to
try to ride past them, turn to **261**.

If you wish to refuse politely their offer and attempt
to enter the town by the north gate, turn to **137**.

10

A jovial man, with long strands of hair hanging down
from the point of his chin, lies in a hammock
suspended at the end of the gangplank. One eye
pops open as you walk on to the deck and, as quick as
a flash, he jumps down and produces a fistful of
tickets from his breast pocket.

'Welcome aboard the *Kazonara*,' he says excitedly,
'the best river boat that ever sailed the Storn.' You
glance back at the board and note the prices: 10 Gold
Crowns to Luyen, 15 to Rhem and 20 to Eula.

'We leave at midnight, sir, so's you best be
a'boarding your horse in the hold without delay.'
Once you have decided which ticket you wish to buy,
pay the man and erase the Gold Crowns from your
Action Chart. Mark the ticket as a Special Item that
you keep in your pocket.

Turn to **82**.

11 – *Illustration I*

The town of Eula has been turned into a huge army
encampment, its people having long since fled to the
north, abandoning their homes and livestock to the
gold-hungry soldiers. Soldiers from a dozen different
nations rub shoulders with fighters of a less-than-
human origin, united by their common greed. As you
watch endless columns of soldiers marching towards

I. The town of Eula has been turned into a huge army encampment

the pall of black smoke rising in the south, your heart begins to sink. The city in which the Lorestone lies, Tekaro, is a city under siege, a city that can withstand the onslaught of ten thousand fighting men. As you ride across the soot-blackened fields towards the siege works and entrenchments at the bank of the River Quarl, you curse the war that threatens to defeat your quest.

Turn to **280**.

12

The arrow thuds into its right leg causing it to shriek and lose its footing. Your quick thinking has bought you enough time to unsheathe a hand weapon and attack the monster.

Yawshath: COMBAT SKILL 22   ENDURANCE 32

Because the creature is now lying face down, do not deduct any ENDURANCE points you may lose in the first two rounds of combat.

You may evade combat at any time by escaping through the arch by which you entered the chapel.

If you wish to evade combat, turn to **305**.
If you win the combat, turn to **112**.

13

Expertly you move through the undergrowth without making a sound until you come to the edge of a small, rocky clearing. A group of ten hooded men stand in a circle around an altar stone. Their leader, a tall thin man wearing a hideous mask of green glass, spins a golden rod around the head of a gigantic toad-like creature spreadeagled on the altar. Lightning writhes like a sparking serpent around the creature's body and, as the chanting rises in pitch, the beast's body floats upwards, hovering in mid-air a few feet above the altar.

Suddenly, the leader shrieks with anger and turns in your direction. He has somehow detected your presence and you feel his blazing fury. He points the golden rod towards you and a charge of energy snakes through the air.

If you have a bow and wish to use it, turn to **56**.

If you do not have a bow and wish to flee, turn to **182**.

If you wish to draw your weapon and prepare for combat, turn to **295**.

14

Suddenly, the riders appear and spread out in a semicircle to surround you. 'We have a debt to settle, northlander,' hisses Roark, his lips drawn back from his teeth in a contemptuous sneer. 'I demand payment in full!'

Madness flashes in his glaring eyes as he removes an amulet from around his neck and holds it high in the air.

'Come, come Tagazin, I summon thee. From the pit of eternal pain, I summon thee!'

The skin on your arms and neck prickles with dread at the sound of Roark's terrible invocation and you cast your eyes around you for an escape route. Only the churchyard offers a way past Roark and his men but, as you spur your horse through the stone gateway, you are suddenly frozen with terror by what you see before you.

Turn to **270**.

15

The town watch gasp in unison, shocked by the seemingly effortless ease with which you have defeated their sergeant. They hesitate and step back, anxious to avoid your gaze and your displeasure. Touching your horse's flanks with your spurs, you move rapidly forward towards the wagons where a handful of fresh-faced guards scatter like frightened chickens. No one dares to challenge you as you manouevre your horse around them and canter along the winding alley ahead.

Turn to **332**.

16

In the dim glow of a street lantern, you unfold the Map of Varetta and study the complicated network of roads and alleys. Mark this as a Special Item on your *Action Chart*. Brass Street is located on the far side of the city, close to the west wall. Suddenly, a bell tolls, its dull clang echoing among the rooftops and towers. It is the curfew: everyone must be off the streets within one hour. You will never reach the far side of the city in an hour, so you resolve to find a tavern for the night and resume your quest at dawn.

Turn to **135**.

17

You walk to the bar and arrange a room for the night. There are many rooms, each of a different standard and price. A blackboard suspended from the ceiling shows the tariffs:

DORMITORY – 2 Gold Crowns a night

SINGLE ROOM (second class) – 3 Gold Crowns a night

SINGLE ROOM (with hot bath) – 5 Gold Crowns a night

You may choose to stay in any of the above rooms, but remember to erase the relevant number of Gold Crowns from your *Action Chart* before turning to your chosen number.

If you decide to stay in the dormitory, turn to **144**.

If you decide to stay in the second-class single room, turn to **202**.

If you decide to stay in the single room with a bath, turn to **251**.

18

On a table in the centre of the tent lies a stack of bows that have been provided by the villagers. Most of them are in very poor condition but you manage to find three that are neither warped, split or unstrung. One is a Vassagonian bow called a Jakan; another is a bone bow from Kalte; and the third is a Durenese hunting bow.

If you decide to take the Jakan, turn to **298**.

If you decide to take the bone bow, turn to **214**.

If you decide to take the Durenese hunting bow, turn to **60**.

If you have the Magnakai Discipline of Hunt-mastery, turn to **205**.

19

Luyen, the city of flowers and wine, greets you, its towers, timbered houses and fortified perimeter walls silhouetted against the sky. It lies in the shadow of the Ceners, at a dangerous bend where the fast-flowing Storn undercuts the sheer slopes of Mount Prindar.

The captain docks at the Luyen quay for provisions and, as his men busy themselves with a myriad of duties and tasks, you accompany him on a visit to the Luyen apothecary.

The entrance to this famed establishment is marked by a huge stone jar, creaking on its chains. The shop is vast, and full of things that stir your curiosity. Towers of containered liquids, mountains of coarse-grained powders and forests of roots and herbs crowd the bleached wooden shelves. The captain seeks medicines of strength and healing in readiness for the battle ahead, and the herbmaster's eyes widen with delight when he reads the captain's list – they are his most expensive preparations.

If you wish to examine some of the potions that line the shelves, turn to **2**.

If you wish to take a look at some of the other shops in this street while the herbmaster prepares the captain's order, turn to **152**.

20

Your ambush catches the enemy by surprise, making them panic and fly in all directions. At such close range your arrow pierces the chainmailed chest of the rider holding Cyrilus's horse and kills him instantly. As he tumbles to the ground, you break cover, exploding through the bushes and scooping the reins from the dead man's horse. Angry shouts echo in your wake as you take off along the highway with the wizard and his horse by your side.

Turn to **188**.

21

At the end of a cool grey marble corridor, you find yourself at the library door. The brown-robed men you saw earlier when you entered the courtyard have all vanished: the hall is now deserted and as quiet as the grave.

The library, too, is empty, save for the thousands of books that line the stone shelves. On the far side of the room there is another door – the only other exit from the library.

If you wish to examine some of the books, turn to **302**.
If you wish to enter the other door, turn to **127**.

22

The gleaming pikeheads are barely inches from your chest when you unsheathe your weapon and smash them aside. Your blow shatters their shafts and the guards reel back, wide-eyed and slack-jawed with shock. Seizing your advantage, you spur your horse once more and gallop towards the welcoming shadows of the street ahead. As the outraged cries of the gatehouse guard fade away, you find yourself at a fork in the road. Shadows are lengthening as night draws its cloak around the border town, and you are anxious to find safe lodging for yourself and your horse.

If you wish to take the left fork, turn to **151**.
If you wish to take the right fork, turn to **289**.
If you have the Magnakai Discipline of Divination, turn to **41**.

23

Your arrow whistles past his shoulder and buries itself in another man's leg as he tries to jump from the ship's rail. If you have another weapon you must unsheathe it, for the pirate is still advancing.

Turn to **92**.

24

The chapel has lain derelict for many years, exposed to the elements. Very little has survived. In one corner you discover a gaping hole that opens on to another room below. Its floor is covered with large shiny black puddles and the overpowering stench of mould and decay is carried upwards by a howling draught. A rat sits on the remains of a corpse, staring up at you in surprise, the dull green light of the chapel reflecting in its peppercorn eyes. As you become accustomed to the gloom, you realize that this room is, in fact, full of corpses: the unfortunate victims of the Yawshath. Then your gaze is drawn to a gleaming bronze warhammer that lies across the chest of a corpse.

Everything below is covered in mould except for this weapon which still shines as if it were brand new.

> If you have a rope you can attempt to retrieve the warhammer by turning to **101**.
> If you would rather ignore the weapon and return to Cyrilus, turn to **338**.
> If you have the Magnakai Discipline of Nexus, turn to **276**.

25

Beyond the doorway, a flight of narrow stone steps leads to a small room. Books line two of the walls from floor to ceiling, and another wall is filled with racks of scrolls, hand bells, and parchments bound round with ribbons of green silk. Then, in the remaining wall, a door opens and a tiny creature with unblinking crimson eyes bids you welcome. Instantly you recognize the stunted features of a Kloon.

'Good evening, sir,' it says in a strong voice that belies its small, squat body. 'Welcome to our guildhouse. How may we be of service?'

> If you wish to ask the Kloon for directions to Brass Street, turn to **165**.
> If you wish to ask it about the Lorestone of Varetta, turn to **262**.
> If you do not wish to question the creature, you may leave the guildhouse and turn to **105**.

26– *Illustration II*

Your score qualifies you for a place in the final, for only one other archer has scored more than eight points. His name is Altan, a tall man with rugged features, a ranger from the mountains to the north. He wields a longbow of orange toa-wood and his skill with this weapon is formidable; it will be a difficult contest.

Altan:

COMBAT SKILL 30   ENDURANCE (TARGET points) 50

The tournament final is played out using the normal rules for combat. The only difference is that you begin with 50 ENDURANCE or TARGET points. Any ENDURANCE points that you may lose are deducted from these TARGET points (your normal ENDURANCE score remaining unchanged throughout the contest). The first one to lose all 50 of his TARGET points loses the tournament. (You need not erase any arrows from your *Action Chart* during this tournament.)

> If you are the first to lose all 50 TARGET points, turn to **183**.
> If Altan is the first to lose all 50 TARGET points, turn to **252**.

27

Spurring your horse up the steep path to the manor house, you pass beneath its turreted gate and halt at a small outhouse whose walls are embellished with intricate ironwork. The top half of a stable door swings open and a spiky-haired youth leers at you.

'Be wantin' a Cess for Amory?' he says offhandedly. 'Three Gold Crowns.'

II.   Altan wields a longbow of orange toa wood

He holds a square of blue card in one hand and presents an open palm with the other.

> If you wish to ask him what a 'Cess' is, turn to **273**.
> If you wish to pay him 3 Gold Crowns, turn to **304**.
> If you decide to ignore him and continue along the highway, turn to **146**.

28

As the warrior crashes to the ground, you see your travelling companion embroiled in a struggle with five armoured horsemen. They have him surrounded and his attempts to free himself are shortlived and futile. A blow from a mace ends all resistance and he falls limply across the neck of his horse. A moment later, the riders gallop away across the bridge with their unconscious captive in tow.

> If you wish to pursue them, turn to **39**.
> If you wish to search the body of your dead enemy, turn to **139**.

29

Blinding pain rips through your chest and thigh as arrows pierce your skin. You scream with shock but the pain quickly gives way to a terrifying numbness. As your horse carries you on towards the Tekaro gate, your last sight is of the tilting cauldrons full of boiling oil and molten lead.

Your life and your quest end here.

30

The three men exchange wary glances before offering you a seat. A pock-marked warrior snaps his fingers and shouts across the crowded hall: 'Wench! four flagons of ale!'

Beer is drawn into four large earthenware vessels, each of which hold half a gallon of ale. Staggering beneath their weight, the serving girl finally arrives and places the flagons on the table.

'Eight Gold Crowns, sir,' she says, breathlessly, the perspiration standing out on her freckled brow.

If you wish to pay for the ale, turn to **230**.
If you cannot or do not want to pay for the ale, turn to **159**.

31

The memory of the dead woman's face flashes into your mind as you stare into Roark's eyes, glitteringly black beneath his wide-brimmed hat. The resemblance is so striking – the same aquiline nose and sallow flesh – that they must be related.

Suddenly, the riders appear and spread out in a semicircle to surround you. A voice shouts, 'Arla is dead – the northlander killed her!'

The lordling's face is transformed into a mask of trembling hatred. Madness flashes in his eyes as he rips open the front of his tunic and tears an amulet from a black chain around his throat.

'Come, come, Tagazin, I summon thee. From the pit of eternal pain I summon thee!'

The skin on your arms and neck prickles with fear as you hear Roark's terrible invocation. You cast your eyes around you for an escape route; only the churchyard offers a way past the lordling and his men. However, as you spur your horse through the stone gateway, you are frozen with terror by what lies ahead.

Turn to **270**.

32

You sense that the strands are living organisms, a sensitive and sophisticated trap to ensnare food for some unknown predator. To continue in this direction could prove fatal.

If you wish to draw the strands aside before you pass through, turn to **4**.

If you decide to go back to the junction and take a different channel, turn to **64**.

33

A shock awaits you on your return to Cyrilus: both he and your horse have vanished. At first you curse him, thinking that he has wandered off to a nearby ale tent for a drink, but when you discover his oaken staff lying beside the road, you sense that something is seriously wrong.

You climb to the top of a parked wagon and strain your eyes in all directions for some clue to his where-abouts. Suddenly you see him, surrounded by a group of cavalrymen galloping away to the west. You count six of them plus a riderless horse – your horse. Then you notice that conveniently hitched to the back of the parked wagon is a saddled horse.

If you wish to take the horse and give chase, turn to **271**.

If you wish to try to find the horse's owner and offer to buy it, turn to **325**.

34

The sound of fighting has drawn the attention of many of the mercenaries and their captains. They hang out of the windows and cheer loudly as you dispatch the last of the city watch. You wipe your weapon and noticing a full purse in the pocket of a dead guard, you take it for yourself. (Pick a number from the *Random Number Table* and add 5 to it: this equals the number of Gold Crowns inside the purse.)

Suddenly, the doors of the tavern open and a mercenary captain ushers you inside before more guards arrive to discover your handiwork. He is very impressed by your fighting prowess and offers to buy you a drink. You sense that it is an honest gesture of friendship without any hidden threat and gratefully accept his offer.

Turn to **211**.

35

You collect your key and climb the stairs to your room at the top of the tavern. You sleep deeply and at dawn rise from your narrow bed to shiver in the fresh breeze whistling through a cracked window pane. As the harsh light of morning floods the tiny garret, you see to your dismay that your Backpack lies half-open on the floor. A gaping hole has been gnawed from the flap: the unmistakable handiwork of rats. Any Meals you had in your backpack have been eaten or ruined. Erase them from your *Action Chart* before leaving the tavern and collecting your horse.

Turn to **272**.

36

You are a few feet from the wagon when your horse refuses the jump. It rears up, its forelegs scrabbling at the air. The long day's ride has taken its toll and your horse has neither the strength nor will left to clear such a daunting obstacle.

You lurch backwards, falling over the horse's rump, and desperately cling to the tightening reins as it teeters on its hind hooves. Suddenly, the horse falls, pinning you beneath her as she crashes to the ground.

Agonizing pain gives way to numbness as you fight to hang on to life, but it is a battle that you can no longer win.

Your life and your quest end here.

37

Suddenly, the taxidermist jumps up from behind a workbench to your right and hurls a glass flask at your face. You dodge instinctively but the flask smashes against your shoulder, showering you with broken glass and burning acid. You lose 12 ENDURANCE points.

If you survive this terrible attack, the taxidermist unsheathes a rapier and lunges at your heart.

Chanda the Taxidermist:
COMBAT SKILL 17   ENDURANCE 24

If you wish to evade combat at any time by running from the shop, mounting your horse and galloping away, turn to **279**.

If you stay and win the combat, turn to **8**.

38

You vault the parapet with barely seconds to spare and tumble into the cold rushing waters of the River Quarl. You are alive but are being swept away from the bridge by the river's irrisistible current.

Turn to **306**.

39

The chase takes you deep into the heart of the Varettian hills. Soon the highway dips and twists, plunging into the valleys and hollows carved by fast-flowing streams, and climbing through the dense woodland that clings precariously to every precipice and crag. You often lose sight of the riders, but your basic Kai skills of tracking and hunting enable you to follow their trail with ease. It is not until you reach a tiny village perched on the edge of a tree-lined crag that their trail becomes indistinct. However, you notice that at the far side of the village, a stony hill track branches from the main highway and ascends into the trees.

If you wish to continue along the highway, turn to **143**.

(contd over)

If you wish to follow the hill track, turn to **241**.
If you have the Magnakai Discipline of Pathsmanship, turn to **117**.

40

You wipe your weapon on the cloak of a dead grave-robber and turn him over with the toe of your boot. Several graves bear the signs of the grave-robbers' labour; the freshly-dug soil is heaped high and coffin lids lie shattered and discarded everywhere. The weapons these men have used are old and pitted with rust and obviously acquired, like the rest of their booty, from graves and tombs. A search of the bodies reveals 27 Gold Crowns, a Bottle of Wine and a Mirror. You may take any of these items before leaving the churchyard.

Turn to **191**.

41

You sense that the left fork harbours a hostile or dangerous force. You cannot identify its exact nature but the aura of wickedness and malevolence is very strong.

If you wish to investigate what lies beyond the left fork, turn to **151**.
If you wish to avoid the obvious presence of evil and take the right fork, turn to **289**.

42

The conditions inside the tent are appalling. Badly wounded men lie on the muddy ground with nothing but rags to dress their injuries. Many are without boots, which have been stolen by their treacherous comrades, who take advantage of their helplessness. One such man is cutting the purse from an unconscious soldier when you enter the hut. He leaps to his feet and attacks you with a curved knife.

   Thief: COMBAT SKILL 16   ENDURANCE 21

If you wish to evade combat at any time by jumping on your horse and galloping off along the path, turn to **70**.

If you win the combat, turn to **86**.

43

There is no reply. You walk round the counter and peer into the back room, but this is also deserted. Your suspicion is aroused when you notice that the oven door and the back door to the hut are both wide open. A rocking chair is lying on its side and there is other evidence of a recent struggle. You are about to search the room when you hear a faint cry for help. It is Cyrilus – he is in trouble.

Turn to **317**.

44

Suddenly, there is a tremendous jolt and you are thrown head first against the rail (lose 2 ENDURANCE points). The screech of twisting metal and splintering wood tears through the silence as the *Kazonara* shudders and dips violently. The boat has hit a boom – a line of logs chained together across the river.

Turn to **224**.

45

It is Altan. Before you can explain what has happened, he shakes your hand and congratulates you on your prowess with a bow for, in spite of his defeat, he is eager to show that he bears no grudge. You thank him and go on to explain your sorry predicament.

'I think we can make a deal,' he says, his eyes glancing at your silver bow.

If you wish to exchange your newly won prize for Altan's horse, turn to **212**.

If you do not wish to part with your silver bow, turn to **148**.

46

A trickle of blood seeps from the corner of the old man's mouth as his eyes flicker and close. He is dead. You bury him in the graveyard of the church where he fell and say a silent prayer to the spirits of the Kai to watch over him on his final journey. A sadness fills your heart and you take one last look at the oaken staff that marks his grave before setting off on the highway to Varetta.

Turn to **168**.

47 – Illustration III

'How dare you waste my time,' he snorts contemptuously. 'Get rid of this fool!'

His bodyguards step forward, their arms raised for attack. You see that one of them is wearing a spiked knuckleduster and, judging by the expression on his face, he is eager to make use of it.

III. One of them is wearing a spiked knuckleduster

Bodyguards: COMBAT SKILL 18   ENDURANCE 34

Due to the speed of their attack you cannot make use of a bow.

If you win the fight, turn to **263**.

48

The hall is soon bustling with noise and activity; tavern brawls are so commonplace in Quarlen that once over they are soon forgotten. The innkeeper's son appears and orders the bodies to be dumped in the river, but not before he relieves them of their purses. 'For breakages,' he says with a snigger.

Lying by your feet is a slim leather tube. You discover that it contains 5 Gold Crowns and a Map of Tekaro, a city to the south. You may keep any of these items. If you wish to keep the map, mark it on your *Action Chart* as a Backpack Item.

If you wish to take a seat and order some food, turn to **172**.

If you wish to approach the bar and ask about a room for the night, turn to **232**.

49

The guard snatches the square of blue card from between your fingers then walks over to a spluttering wall torch, which he removes from its bracket. Holding the torch high, he returns and examines first the card and then your face.

'Enter,' he snarls, crumpling the card in his hairy fist. You flick your heel and urge your tired horse through the town gate.

Turn to **129**.

50

They cannot both be speaking the truth, for the conjurer said that at least one of them was lying. Unfortunately, you have lost your wager.

Erase the Gold Crowns you staked on the conundrum from your *Action Chart* before approaching the bar and enquiring about a room for the night.

Turn to **253**.

51

You gasp as the blade gashes your hip before sinking several inches into the wooden parapet (you lose 2 ENDURANCE points). The pirate is unnerved by the fact that you are still alive and is off balance as you scramble forward and attack. Before he can recover, he is tumbling backwards over the side into the cold, deep waters of the Storn.

Turn to **254**.

52

A hail of arrows engulfs you; pain explodes through your chest, neck and shoulder. You are mortally wounded and although you fight with grim determination to hang on to life, it is a struggle you cannot win. Weak from shock and loss of blood, you fall from the saddle and die on the highway to Varetta.

Your life and your quest end here.

53

The man listens to your question while his eyes try to fathom your purpose.

54

'And what would a warrior be seeking in the Street of the Sages, I wonder?' he muses, his slim fingers stroking his long grey beard.

You are trying to think of a good answer that will not reveal the nature of your quest when the man suddenly becomes agitated.

'I cannot help you,' he says curtly and hurries away from the bar, vanishing into the crowds of drunken mercenaries in the blink of an eye. You are puzzled by his sudden departure – was it something you said that caused him to behave so strangely?

Unless you have already done so, if you wish to approach the merchant at his table, turn to **240**.

If you would rather approach the tavern-keeper, turn to **312**.

54

You have little choice but to spend the night in the stable with your horse. Your sleep is very uncomfortable, for the stable is both draughty and damp. You lose 2 ENDURANCE points. Make the necessary adjustments to your *Action Chart*.

Turn to **272**.

55

'Bah!' exclaims a guard contemptuously. 'We have no time for witless wanderers. Go back to Casiorn if you have no business here.' He spits at the ground and the guards turn towards the open town gate.

  If you wish to offer them gold to let you enter, turn to **9**.

  If you wish to ride past them and through the open gate, turn to **261**.

  If you decide to turn away and attempt to enter the town by the north gate, turn to **137**.

56

You draw an arrow, aim and fire a split second before the bolt of energy hits your chest. Your arrow pierces the leader's heart, killing him instantly, but the wound that you yourself suffer knocks you to the ground. Pick a number from the *Random Number Table*. The number you have picked equals the number of ENDURANCE points that you have lost due to the chest wound.

If you are still alive, you scramble to your feet and run as fast as you can through the undergrowth towards your horse. The golden rod has been retrieved by one of the other men and he is preparing to use it again.

  Turn to **182**.

57

The bolt hits you with such force that you are lifted out of the saddle and thrown to the ground. Flashing lights spin before your eyes and you gasp for breath as a terrifying numbness spreads from your chest through your limbs. There is no pain – only a chilling paralysis that robs you of all resistance to death.

Your quest and your life end here at the Denka Gate.

58

You sense that the Kloon is deeply insulted and has gone to fetch his pet: a very ferocious Vassagonian warhound. As the warhound has not been fed for over two days, it is very unlikely that it will listen to reason. Without a moment's hesitation, you decide to leave the guildhouse before the Kloon and his hungry hound return.

Turn to **105**.

59

You sense that the time has come for you to decide whether to stay with the captain or to leave his company and ride to Tekaro alone.

If you wish to stay with the captain, turn to **290**.
If you decide to ride to Tekaro alone, turn to **11**.

60

The quality of the weapons made by Durenese armourers has justly made them famous throughout the Lastlands. The bow you have chosen is very old but unlike the other two bows it is still in excellent working order.

To begin the tournament, turn to **340**.

61

Your Magnakai Discipline makes you sensitive to the faintest aroma of gallowbrush. It is commonly called 'Sleeptooth' in your homeland of Sommerlund, for the crushed thorns of the gallowbrush briar make a very powerful sleeping draught. For some unknown reason, this man is trying to make you unconscious.

If you wish to draw your weapon and attack him, turn to **277**.

If you wish to throw down your goblet and leave, turn to **279**.

62

You are correct: the boy has blond hair and the girl has black hair. Your logical thinking revealed they could not both have been speaking the truth for the conjurer had said that at least one of them was lying – and if one was lying then the other could not have been speaking the truth. Therefore, there was only one conclusion to be drawn: both lied.

The conjurer pays you the number of Gold Crowns equal to that which you wagered. Remember to add this sum to your current total of Gold Crowns before approaching the bar and enquiring about a room for the night.

Turn to **253**.

63– *Illustration IV (overleaf)*

The path that leads to Castle Taunor is steep and slippery, and far too treacherous to be attempted on horseback. Cyrilus offers to stay and look after your horse while you collect some spa water, saying that

IV.   The path to Castle Taunor is steep and slippery

he is too old to climb the hill track. However, you suspect that it is just his excuse to take an afternoon nap.

The castle is less than a mile from the highway, yet it takes over half an hour to complete the hazardous climb to the rock shelf. The crumbling castle walls are covered with damp foliage and mildew, and the overhanging precipice envelops the keep with its gloomy shadow. You follow the sound of dripping water until you find yourself in a small chapel, where you discover a rivulet of sparkling spa-water trickling from a crack in the altar stone. As you kneel at the altar, filling your glass jar, you suddenly hear a noise: you are not alone.

If you have the Magnakai Discipline of Huntmastery, turn to **162**.

If you do not possess this skill, turn to **278**.

64

You retrace your steps to the junction and pause so that you can decide which is the best route to take.

If you wish to go straight ahead, turn to **339**.

If you decide to take the channel to your left, turn to **269**.

65

With a blood-curdling shriek, the Yawshath dives straight for you from the top of the stairs. With ice-cold nerve you steel yourself to strike. Your blow is well timed and deadly accurate, tearing open the creature's chest. A split second later you leap aside to avoid being crushed beneath its heavy body as it crashes into the flagstones. It shudders for a brief moment before death comes to claim its evil soul.

Shaken, but thankful to be alive, you return to the chapel and fill your glass jar with Taunor Water (there is enough spa water to restore 6 ENDURANCE points). You may drink the water now or store it in your Backpack for future use. If you do keep it, mark it on your *Action Chart* as a Backpack Item.

If you now wish to search the chapel, turn to **24**.
If you decide to return to Cyrilus, turn to **338**.

66

The man is quick to react to your attack. Hurling the silver tray at your head, he escapes through a curtained archway at the back of the shop.

If you wish to give chase, turn to **324**.
If you decide to let him go and leave the taxidermy, turn to **279**.

67

The street becomes as silent as death as all eyes focus accusingly on you. The leader's face becomes twisted with hatred. He points a crooked finger at your forehead and utters a dreadful curse.

If you have the Magnakai Discipline of Psi-screen, turn to **255**.
If you do not possess this skill, turn to **315**.

68

As you ride along the quay, you study your map of the Stornlands for an alternative route to Tekaro. There are two roads that will take you there: the mountain highway through the Ceners via Rhem, or the valley highway through Amory and the forest of Eula. Lack of sleep and fatigue from your long ride cloud your mind and you decide that your first priority must be to have a good night's sleep.

A quayside tavern displays a sign promising the most comfortable beds in all of Soren. This is all you need to be persuaded to stable your horse and enter its doors.

Turn to **167**.

69

You press yourself into the narrow recess and pray that the creature will pass you by. Pick a number from the *Random Number Table*. If you have the Magnakai Discipline of Invisibility, add 5 to the number you have picked.

If your total is now *0—5*, turn to **128**.
If it is now *6—14*, turn to **246**.

70

The path ends at the point where the Rivers Storn and Quarl converge in a V-shaped bank. Ogron engineers and carpenters are busy at work constructing pontoons for floating bridges, which look like enclosed rowing boats and are destined to be used to cross the river further downstream.

Staring out across the water, you notice a dark shadow like the entrance to a cave at the base of the city wall. After concentrating for a few moments, you find you can make out the dull criss-cross of metal bars. It is a sewer outfall.

If you wish to ask the blue-skinned Ogrons what they know about the sewer outfall, turn to **133**.

If you wish to try to take one of the pontoons and row across the river, turn to **163**.

If you wish to swim across the river, turn to **171**.

71– *Illustration V*

The man leaps back, unsheathing a wide-bladed sword from beneath his bearskin cloak. 'Fool!' he cries, contemptuously. 'Victory to the man who is left alive.' You have insulted this man and he is determined to fight you to the death as a matter of honour. If you have the Magnakai Discipline of Animal Control you may add 2 points to your COMBAT SKILL for the duration of the fight as you are fighting from the saddle.

Redbeard: COMBAT SKILL 19   ENDURANCE 28

If you wish to evade combat at any time by galloping along the street, turn to **279**.

If you win the combat, turn to **237**.

72

The shouts of the town guard sergeant ring in your ears as you urge your horse towards the wagon. You pray that your mount has strength enough to clear the obstacle, for you are now committed to jumping it – you cannot turn back.

Pick a number from the *Random Number Table*. If you have the Magnakai Discipline of Animal Control, add 2 to the number you have picked.

If your total is now *0—1*, turn to **36**.

If your total is now *2—7*, turn to **166**.

If your total is now *8—11*, turn to **274**.

V. He is determined to fight you to the death

73

Shortly before noon you pass through a deserted village. The burnt-out ruins of cottages and farm-steads dot the landscape like charred skeletons – the unmistakable signs of war. A mile or two farther along the highway you come across a church. A man, his clothes ragged and covered with mud, is moving amongst the gravestones, staggering like a wounded carrion crow. As you reach the church gate, he sees you and cries out pitifully for help.

If you wish to help the man, turn to **337**.

If you do not wish to help the man and would rather ignore him and continue riding towards Soren, turn to **191**.

If you have the Magnakai Discipline of Curing, turn to **173**.

74

You do not have to wait very long for the riders to appear. As soon as they think you have gone, they emerge in single file from the back of a derelict cottage and draw themselves into a circle in the middle of the village. Although they are out of ear-shot, you can tell by their frantic movements and gestures that they are having a heated argument. Suddenly, they break the circle and ride towards you. Cyrilus, still lying unconscious across his horse, is in tow behind the last rider.

If you have a bow and want to ambush them as they ride past your hiding place, turn to **20**.

If you wish to attack the last rider and try to recapture Cyrilus, turn to **203**.

If you wish to let them pass and then follow them, turn to **227**.

75

A deafening roar of rage and pain fills your ears. The monster staggers back, its face transformed into a bloody scarlet mask as the arrow pierces its eye. It shudders and sways before keeling over on to its back, writhing for a brief moment in the mud and debris of the chapel floor.

Turn to **112**.

76

It is customary for the proprietor of the Inn of the Crossed Swords to throw out anyone who cannot pay his board and lodging. This makes your position difficult as the curfew bell was rung nearly an hour ago and anyone found in the streets an hour after its sounding is liable to be imprisoned by the city watch.

Rather than face imprisonment and the possible failure of your quest, you can sell some of your equipment in order to raise cash. The fat-bellied mercenary who took your bets will pay the following prices for these (but only these) Items:

> SWORD – 3 Gold Crowns
> DAGGER – 1 Gold Crown
> BROADSWORD – 6 Gold Crowns
> SHORT SWORD – 2 Gold Crowns
> MACE – 3 Gold Crowns
> RUBY RING – 10 Gold Crowns
> WARHAMMER – 5 Gold Crowns
> SPEAR – 4 Gold Crowns
> AXE – 2 Gold Crowns
> BOW – 5 Gold Crowns
> QUARTERSTAFF – 2 Gold Crowns
> SILVER BROOCH – 7 Gold Crowns

(contd over)

You will need a minimum of 2 Gold Crowns in order to stay the night at the Inn of the Crossed Swords.

If you wish to sell him some equipment, make the necessary adjustments to your *Action Chart* and turn to **336**.

If you wish to keep your equipment, or do not have items of interest to the mercenary, you must take your chances with the city watch and turn to **138**.

77 – *Illustration VI*

Leaping over the dead bodies, you fight your way across the deck to where the captain is in combat with five pirates. While he attacks with a longsword in his right hand, he parries enemy cutlasses with a bronze sleeve-shield that encases his left forearm. He fights with cool determination, making light work of the battle-clumsy pirates. Then a war horn heralds the arrival of a new and formidable wave of attackers. You anticipate the captain's danger and rush to protect his back from the snarling, mad-eyed pirate berserkers.

Pirate Berserkers:
COMBAT SKILL 20   ENDURANCE 30

Due to their state of battle frenzy, the pirate berserkers are immune to Mindblast, but *not* Psi-surge.

If you win the combat, turn to **297**.

78

You prepare yourself for combat and leap to the defence of the helpless old man just in time to turn aside the lordling's sword.

VI.   You rush to protect the captain from the snarling pirate
berserkers

'Curse you, scum!' he cries. 'I am Roark, highborn of Amory. How dare you interfere with my sport.'

He feints withdrawal but you are not taken in by his street-brawl tactics. As his sword cuts the air in a vicious back-handed slash, you are ready to parry the blow. The tavern crowd cheer in anticipation of a good fight.

Roark: COMBAT SKILL 24   ENDURANCE 30

If you reduce Roark's ENDURANCE to 11 points or less, do not continue the combat but turn instead to **180**.

79

You pass many soldiers of different races and nationalities, lolling in open doorways or squatting against the red brick walls. They are mercenaries, drawn to Varetta by the news of war in the north. They come in search of employment, for the chance to sell their skills to any buyer, indifferent to the justness of his cause.

Beneath a black iron lantern, you notice a group of men throwing dice against the side of a wall.

If you wish to stop and ask them the way to Brass Street, turn to **291**.

If you wish to continue on your way, turn to **307**.

80

The flame illuminates a deep circular pit where the floor of the chamber should be. Lying at the bottom are a myriad of human skulls and bones, their surfaces strangely smooth and yellow as if corroded by some powerful acid. The faintest of sounds makes you glance over your shoulder – you are frozen with terror by the sight that meets your eyes. A huge lumbering monster fills the tunnel, over ten feet tall with thick, twisted limbs and eight-fingered hands tipped with razor-sharp talons that are poised to rip your flesh. Baleful, monstrous eyes protrude from yellow slits in its glistening head, and a long reptillian tail whips behind it.

It strikes before you can react, knocking you back into the pit. A peculiar and hideous sound fills the chamber as it claws a lever in the wall, causing a rain of yellow fluid to pour from the ceiling. As the acid eats through your cloak and sears your flesh, the last thing you hear is the hideous laughter of the Dakomyd.

Your quest and your life end here in the sewers of Tekaro.

81

Arrows scream past on all sides. One shaft gouges a furrow of skin from the horse's rump, causing him to twist and buck; you shorten the reins and urge him forward. Your quick thinking helps you regain control of the frightened animal and soon you are well out of range of the deadly arrows.

Turn to **39**.

82

The hold of the riverboat is full of horses; not the slow carthorses favoured by merchants, but strong and sturdy mounts that carry many scars of battle upon their muscular flanks. You unsaddle your mare, load her manger with feed and then make your way back on deck.

As you emerge from the hold, a voice calls out to you and you raise your weary eyes. It is the captain – the mercenary leader you ran across at the Inn of the Crossed Swords.

'Well met, my friend,' he cries and slaps you enthusiastically on the shoulder. 'So you changed your mind! You have come to join my band of fearless fighters.' Before you have a chance to answer, the captain and his men, who are all considerably the worse for drink, stumble past on a quest of the utmost importance – the search for the wine store. You are far too tired and weary to follow – the thought of your cabin bed and a good night's sleep is all that interests you.

Turn to **341**.

The old man narrows his mousy eyes and looks at you with a cautious stare. 'It is but a legend. Some say it contained great power; others say its power existed only in the minds of those who craved to own it. Whatever the truth is, the Lorestone has been lost for hundreds of years.'

You sense that the old magician is not telling you all he knows about the Lorestone.

If you wish to identify yourself and tell him the nature of your quest, turn to **119**.

If you choose not to reveal your identity, bid him goodnight and turn to **239**.

84

The taxidermist points to a vat in the corner of the room that contains a noxious blue fluid, which is obviously the source of the unpleasant smell.

'My special preservative,' he says proudly. 'It has taken me many years to perfect the formula but my experiments are now complete. All I require is a specimen worthy of the immortality it can provide.'

The man's voice is beginning to sound faint and distant, as if he were falling away from you into a deep, dark pit. Your eyelids feel heavy and you are having difficulty in concentrating on what he says. Suddenly, you realize that you have been drugged; the wine contained a powerful draught of gallow-brush, although you did not detect it at the time. You fight to remain awake but it is a battle you cannot win, for the enemy is in your very blood. The taxidermist has at last found a specimen worthy of his special preservative – the last of the Kai Lords of Sommerlund.

Your quest and your life end here.

85

As you hear the click of the crossbow trigger, you throw yourself to the ground to avoid the deadly missile. The bolt grazes your scalp (lose 2 ENDURANCE points), and embeds itself in the side of the log hut. A moment later you are back on your feet. The warrior discards his empty weapon and reins his horse about in order to follow the others across the bridge.

If you have a bow, turn to **178**.
If you do not have a bow, you must mount your horse and give chase, and turn to **39**.

86

Prising the pouch from the thief's hand, you return it to the pocket of the unconscious soldier. Many of the wounded men witness what you have done and from that moment you become a hero in their eyes. Your use of the Magnakai Discipline of Curing to heal many of their wounds strengthens their esteem and devotion and they pledge themselves to help you in any way they can.

If you wish to ask them if there is any way of getting into Tekaro undetected, turn to **109**.

If you do not wish to ask them anything and would rather leave, turn to **70**.

87

The town watch rush forward to avenge their sergeant's death but in their haste they leave the gap between the two wagons unprotected. You are quick to notice this opportunity for escape and spur your mount straight for the running guards. These fresh-faced young men have no battle skill – their attack is clumsy and hesitant. You break through them in a matter of seconds and have soon left them far behind as you gallop along the street beyond the wagons.

Turn to **332**.

88

Your speedy dispatch of the robbers has earned you 5 Gold Crowns, which you find in the pockets of the dead men, and the respectful glances of several mercenary captains. One in particular is so impressed by your fighting prowess that he approaches you and offers to buy you a drink. You sense that it is a honest gesture of friendship without any hidden threat, and gratefully accept his offer.

Turn to **211**.

89

'Esmond, you old rascal, show yourself – it's Cyrilus your brother. I've someone with me I want you to meet,' cries the wizard as he raps on the gate with his oaken staff. There is no reply. He smiles and shrugs his bony shoulders before shouting: 'Wake up you old fool, I know you're in there,' but still there is no reply.

If you have the Magnakai Discipline of Divination, turn to **7**.

If you do not possess this skill, turn to **258**.

90

The faintest of sounds makes you glance over your shoulder. You are frozen with abject terror by the sight that greets you. A huge lumbering monster fills the tunnel, over ten feet high with thick twisted limbs and eight-fingered hands tipped with razor-sharp talons that are poised to rip your flesh. Baleful, monstrous eyes protrude from yellow slits in its glistening head and a long reptilian tail whips behind it.

91

Before you can react, it strikes, knocking you back into a pit. A peculiar and hideous sound fills the vault and you feel a hot sticky fluid raining down on your head. As it eats through your cloak and sears your flesh, the last thing you hear is the hideous laughter of the Dakomyd.

Your quest and your life end here in the sewers of Tekaro.

91

Your curiosity is drawn to a game of cards that is taking place in the centre of the hall. Six ruddy-faced men are gambling against a croupier on the turn of the cards. You are quick to spot that the deck he is using is marked. When a seat is vacated by one of the men, you take his place. The first round is on the house – you need not place a stake.

Needless to say, knowing how the game has been rigged, you win the first round and continue to win several more. Pick a number from the *Random Number Table* and add 5 to it. This equals the number of Gold Crowns that you win before the dealer suspects something is wrong and ends the game.

Now that you have some gold in your pouch once more, if you wish to approach the bar and ask about a room for the night, turn to **232**.

If you wish to take a seat and order some food, turn to **172**.

92

The man shrieks his battle-cry and lashes out with a heavy-bladed cutlass.

Deldenian River Pirate:
COMBAT SKILL 17   ENDURANCE 23

If you wish to evade combat at any time, turn to **286**.

If you win and combat lasts 3 rounds or less, turn to **77**.

If combat lasts longer than 3 rounds, turn to **215**.

93

Taking hold of the man's shoulder, you shake him to try to wake him from his drunken slumber but he keels over and slumps to the floor. The back of his shirt is covered with a huge bloodstain spreading from the handle of a dagger that is buried deep in his spine. As you recoil in horror, you hear a faint cry for help. It is Cyrilus – he is in trouble.

Turn to **317**.

94

Ripping aside the curtain, you rush into a small room full of storage cupboards and work tables. You cast your eyes around the workshop annexe but there is no sign of the man: he has vanished.

If you have the Magnakai Discipline of Divination or Huntmastery, turn to **208**.

If you do not possess either of these skills, turn to **37**.

95

The ghastly sound of the creature's hungry cry chills your blood. It is barely a few feet away when you let loose your arrow.

Pick a number from the *Random Number Table*. If you have the Magnakai Discipline of Weaponmastery with bow, add 3 to the number you have picked.

If your total is now *0—3*, turn to **155**.
If it is *4—12*, turn to **12**.

96

An hour after sunset you arrive at the gates of Amory. Beneath the deepening shadow of its watchful guard tower, you fight back your fatigue and wait as the gate creaks open. A soldier wearing a hauberk of black and gold chainmail, strides forward and demands to see a Cess.

If you possess a Cess, turn to **49**.
If you do not possess this Special Item, turn to **221**.

97

The ambush is so sudden and so swift that only luck can save you now. Pick a number from the *Random Number Table*.

If the number you have chosen is *0—3*, turn to **174**.
If the number is *4—6*, turn to **313**.
If the number is *7—9*, turn to **57**.

98

The smell of dust and rusty metal wafts in your face as you enter the cluttered weapons shop. All manner of arms are stacked in racks that rise precariously to the ceiling. Their prices are chalked on a circular slate that hangs above the counter.

> BROADSWORDS – 7 Gold Crowns
> DAGGERS – 2 Gold Crowns
> SHORT SWORDS – 3 Gold Crowns
> WARHAMMERS – 6 Gold Crowns
> SPEARS – 5 Gold Crowns
> MACES – 4 Gold Crowns
> AXES – 3 Gold Crowns
> BOWS – 7 Gold Crowns
> QUARTERSTAFFS – 3 Gold Crowns
> SWORDS – 4 Gold Crowns
> ARROWS – 2 for 1 Gold Crown

You may purchase any of the above weapons if you have enough money to do so. The shop owner will also buy any weapons that you may already have for 1 Gold Crown *less* than the price shown on the slate. Mark any changes on your *Action Chart* before you leave.

Turn to **275**.

99

You feel a numbing shock and then the damp warmth of blood begins to soak your tunic. You fight for breath but your strength is sapped by the terrible wounds made by the pikeheads. You swoon and fall to the ground through loss of blood, unconscious of the sword blade that is poised to end your life.

Your quest and your life have come to an early and tragic end here.

100– *Illustration VII*

It is late afternoon when you catch your first breath-taking glimpse of Varetta. Built on a massive plateau, this city has stood since time immemorial. The walls and buildings are immense, constructed from blood-red rock and crowded together in complicated splendour. Great stone dragons writhe along the battlements, their coiled tails entangling the gatehouses and portals of the outer wall, and spirals of smoke rise from the mouths of angry-faced gargoyles, crouching like spies on top of the roofs and towers that fill the sky.

The sun has set by the time you reach the east gate. The red-coated guards offer no challenge and you pass into the wide streets of this magnificent city, to arrive eventually at a quadrangle. A pillar of red stone indicates the names of the streets that lead away from the square.

If you wish to go north into Helin Way, turn to **79**.

If you wish to go west into Coachcourse, turn to **135**.

If you wish to go south into Flute Street, turn to **147**.

If you decide to go east, along the street down which you have just ridden, turn to **238**.

101

You make a noose at one end of the rope and lower it carefully through the hole in the floor. If you can slip the noose around the head of the hammer, it should tighten as you pull on the rope and draw the hammer upwards.

VII.   The ancient city of Varetta

Pick a number from the *Random Number Table*. If you have the Magnakai Discipline of Huntmastery, add 3 to the number you have chosen.

If your total is now 0–4, turn to **348**.
If it is 5 or higher, turn to **207**.

102

Night has fallen by the time you reach the river town of Soren and the sky is clear and full of stars that sparkle with icy splendour. You ride the main street towards the quay where a score of river ships lie docked at the town. Their signal lamps, shimmering red and green from the mast-tops, reflect upon the cold, dark waters of the River Storn.

A board standing beside the gangplank to a large transport caravel catches your eye. On it are chalked the prices of passage to three destinations.

> LUYEN – 10 Gold Crowns
> RHEM – 15 Gold Crowns
> EULA – 20 Gold Crowns

A fourth destination – Tekaro – has been crossed out and scribbled beside it is: 'Cancelled due to war'.

If you wish to buy a ticket to one of the destinations, turn to **10**.
If you do not wish to buy a ticket – or cannot afford to – turn to **68**.

103

Unfortunately, your score is too low to qualify for the next round of the contest and you are politely asked to leave the field. If you have been using a borrowed bow, you must return it to the tent before making your way back to Cyrilus.

Turn to **33**.

104

Your thoughts return to your quest and to Cyrilus's dying words. The man he was taking you to meet lives in Brass Street, but in a city the size of Varetta it could take you days to find the right street. You decide to try to find out where it is from someone in the tavern and look around the massive hall in search of a likely source of information.

If you wish to approach a merchant who sits alone at a nearby table, turn to **240**.

If you wish to ask a distinguished-looking man who stands at the bar, turn to **53**.

If you wish to ask the tavern-keeper, turn to **312**.

105

A few hundred yards along the street is the east gate through which you entered the city. Two streets lead away from the gatehouse; one heading north, the other south.

If you wish to go north, turn to **79**.

If you wish to go south, turn to **147**.

106

Painfully, you drag yourself from beneath the dead monster. Several of your ribs are cracked and you have a nasty gash on the back of your head, but at least you are still alive.

You stagger up the stairs and back to the chapel where you fill your glass jar with Taunor Water. (The healing spa water will restore 6 ENDURANCE points.) You may drink the Water now or place the glass jar in your Backpack for future use. If you keep the Taunor Water, mark it on your *Action Chart* as a Backpack Item.

If you wish to search the chapel, turn to **24**.
If you decide to return to Cyrilus, turn to **338**.

107

The trapdoor is heavy and stiff but gradually its seal of rust cracks and loosens under the pressure. Inch by inch you force it open to reveal at last the cobblestoned city square. Across the square, directly ahead, is the cathedral of Tekaro. As the square is teeming with guards, you are forced to close the hatch quickly to avoid being detected.

You estimate that the cathedral is approximately two hundred yards due east. As you descend the steps and continue through the passage, you pray that the sewer will give access to the crypt.

Turn to **120**.

108

You prepare to defend yourself against a sudden attack while trying to give the impression that you are, in fact, relaxing your guard. There is a long pause. before the leader turns his back on you and addresses his followers in a loud, self-righteous tone.

'Witness the power of Vashna, my brothers – his spirit

is alive. Even this ignorant and unworthy stranger acknowledges his presence.'

A doleful lament rises from the procession in praise of their leader. As the ghastly chanting builds up to a fevered climax, you slip into the shadows of an alley and spur your horse away from the sinister worshippers.

Turn to **332**.

109

Some of the men laugh and look at you as though you are crazy, but one man calls you over to his side and hands you a leather tube.

'It's a Map of Tekaro,' he whispers, painfully. 'I . . . I don't know how you can enter the city, but if you do find a way this map may be of use.'

You thank the injured man and leave the tent. Unless you already possess a Map of Tekaro, you may keep this Map. Mark it on your *Action Chart* as a Backpack Item.

Turn to **70**.

110

'None passin' by 'ere,' she says, her voice heavy with a highland accent. 'Track go t' top o' Beacon 'ill an' no mor'n that.' You sense that the old woman is telling the truth: the riders have not come this way and the track leads nowhere – it is a dead end. You thank her and bid her farewell before turning around and descending the track.

Turn to **330**.

111

A yellow velvet pouch hanging from a dead pirate's belt catches your eye. You cut it free and discover that it contains some Potion of Laumspur, a herb with well-known healing properties. This pouch contains enough of the herb to restore 4 lost ENDURANCE points. You may either swallow the Laumspur now, or place it in your Backpack for future use.

Turn to **77**.

112

The creature shudders and its arms jerk, clawing at the air. As it dies, its body twitches with a few final convulsions. You stare down at the hideous carcass but quickly pull away when you notice that its fur is alive with crawling parasites. They know instinctively that their old host is dead and they are abandoning the body in search of a new one.

You hurry over to the altar where you fill your glass jar with Taunor Water. (The healing spa water will restore 6 ENDURANCE points.) You may drink the Water now or place the glass jar in your Backpack for future use. If you do keep it, mark it on your *Action Chart* as a Backpack Item.

If you now wish to search the rest of the chapel, turn to **24**.

If you decide to return to Cyrilus, turn to **338**.

113

This is not the correct answer. The conjurer stated that at least one child was lying and if one lied then the other could not have been telling the truth. The right answer is that both childrn lied, so unfortunately you have lost the gold you wagered.

Erase the Gold Crowns you staked on the conundrum from your *Action Chart*, before approaching the bar and enquiring about a room for the night.

Turn to **253**.

114

You silence the robber's whispered threats, slamming your clenched fist into his throat and at the same time grabbing hold of his tunic with your other hand. He tries to scream but his larynx has been crushed by your blow. He gurgles pitifully as you twist him around to shield yourself as his accomplice lunges with his dagger. It sinks deeply into the robber's heart and, as he slumps to his knees, you draw your own weapon and attack his startled killer. Due to the surprise of your attack, you may add 2 to your COMBAT SKILL for the first round of combat.

Backstabber: COMBAT SKILL 15   ENDURANCE 22

If you win the combat, turn to **88**.

115

The startled guard dives aside as you spur your horse straight for him. You find that the gatehouse arch opens on to a cobblestoned square but the only exit is blocked by the wagon and merchant caravan. A dozen guards, dressed in the green and black tunics of the town watch, are checking their cargoes. As you burst from the shadows of the gatehouse arch, they see you and cry in unison: 'Tollbreaker! Tollbreaker!

If you wish to rein in your horse and prepare to fight the town watch, turn to **248**.

If you wish to attempt to jump over the wagons and escape into the shadows of the winding street ahead, turn to **72**.

116–*Illustration VIII*

Suddenly, the door bursts open and in lopes a ravenous warhound. 'Supper time, Goregasher!' cries the Kloon, gleefully, as the slavering hound leaps at your throat.

Ravenous Warhound:
COMBAT SKILL 17   ENDURANCE 25

You may evade this attack in the first round of combat only, by running from the room and escaping down the stairs to the street.

If you wish to evade combat, turn to **105**.

If you win the fight, turn to **193**.

117

Using your Magnakai Discipline, you examine both the hill path and the highway for recent tracks. To your surprise you discover that neither route has been used by horsemen in the last three hours. It can mean only one thing – the riders are hiding somewhere in the village.

VIII.   'Supper time, Goregasher!' cries the Kloon gleefully

If you wish to ride back into the village, turn to **52**.

If you wish to hide in the trees and wait for the riders to show themselves, turn to **74**.

118

You sleep soundly and then rise an hour after dawn, clear-headed and eager to continue your ride. The morning news from the south is that the mountain highway to Rhem is impassable; an avalanche has destroyed all traces of the road near Mount Navalyn and it will be many weeks before the rubble is cleared and the road rebuilt. This leaves you with only one choice – you must take the valley road through Amory and the forest of Eula.

You gather together your equipment and set off without delay. If you are to reach Amory by sunset you will need to ride at great speed and without a break.

Turn to **96**.

119

Cyrilus' eyes open with such surprise that you can see the startled whites around his mousy-brown pupils. 'Lone Wolf,' he whispers, incredulously, 'I should have known. Humble apologies, my lord. I thought that you sought the Lorestone for less than honourable reasons.'

Cyrilus talks at great length about the legend of the Lorestone. You learn that it remained in Varetta after Sun Eagle's quest, where it was set into the throne of Lyris in the Tower of the King. Hundreds of years ago, during the War of the Lorestone, it was stolen by a Salonese prince called Kaskor. He set the stone upon a gold sceptre and used it in battle to inspire his fanatical followers and crush his foes. He believed it made him invulnerable, but this was not so – he was killed on his royal barge during a battle at Rhem and the Lorestone was lost when the gold sceptre fell from his hand into the depths of the River Storn. There were many accounts of the sceptre having been found but they had always proved to be untrue or simply fanciful. It was said that whoever wielded the Lorestone was the rightful ruler of all the Stornlands. For this reason alone it was often sought by evil or unscrupulous warlords, and many had pursued the quest, all without success.

Cyrilus does not know where the Lorestone is, but he does know a man in Varetta who claims to know its exact whereabouts. 'Let me ride with you to Varetta; in return for the privilege I shall take you to this man.' Your basic Kai instincts tell you his offer is genuine. You nod your agreement and arrange to meet him in the tavern courtyard at dawn.

Turn to **5**.

120

Less than fifty yards along the channel, another passage joins the main flow from the right.

If you wish to investigate this new passage, turn to **339**.

If you wish to press on along the main course, turn to **140**.

121

The shop is filled with a fascinating collection of stuffed creatures, each one in a life-like pose and displayed in a realistic setting. A two-headed wolf stands guard at the entrance to a cave, a baknar lies on a snowy ledge and a desert ganthi drinks its fill from a sculptured oasis of sandstone and toa-trees.

You are examining the beautifully preserved head of an itikar when you hear a soft, cultivated voice behind you.

'Good evening, sir. Welcome to my establishment.'

A tall, aristocratic man dressed in a richly embroidered robe steps forward and bows. He is clearly impressed by your interest in his work and offers to conduct you on a brief tour of his shop.

If you wish to see more of the fascinating taxidermy, turn to **345**.

If you wish to decline his generous offer and leave the shop, turn to **149**.

122

Your senses warn you that a steep drop lies beyond the breach in the castle wall. If you were to run that way, you could be heading for your doom.

If you wish to ignore your instincts and climb through the hole in the castle wall, turn to **217**.

If you wish to run down the stairs towards the iron gate, turn to **169**.

123

A handful of Alether Berries costs 3 Gold Crowns. If you swallow them before a fight they will increase your COMBAT SKILL by 2 points for the duration of the fight. You may purchase up to 3 handfuls of Alether Berries. Each handful counts as one Backpack Item but you cannot swallow more than one handful during any one combat.

When you have concluded your purchases, you remount your horse and leave the village.

Turn to **100**.

124

The city is choked with people: mercenaries from the north and west, weapon merchants from the east and ragged refugees from the war-torn south. The captain orders his men to sleep aboard the *Kazonara* this night, forbidding them to go ashore, for Prince Balonn of Rioma and his mercenary knights are encamped inside the city wall. A bitter and long-standing rivalry exists between the two companies and the captain wisely wishes to avoid any confrontation.

Rumour has it that a number of the Stornland's most powerful princes are gathered in Rhem to plot the defeat of the Slovians. However, the captain believes it is more likely that the robber-barons are conspiring against each other to steal the riches of Tekaro for themselves.

You set sail at first light, bidding farewell to the slender twin-towers of the Rhem citadel, which overshadows the city quay. The Storn flows southwards through steep-sided fields of vines, arranged in endless straight rows like the waves of a green sea. The weather is warm and you spend the day on deck watching the traffic of refugees heading north along a highway, and the strange gigantic toads, the Sloats, at work, pulling riverboats and barges upstream.

It is late afternoon when you sight the town of Eula in the distance. You saddle your horse and shoulder your equipment as the *Kazonara* berths at the town's wooden pier.

If you purchased a Riverboat Ticket for the riverboat at Soren, turn to **59**.

If you do not have a Riverboat Ticket, turn to **290**.

125

The soldiers are swilling ale and reminiscing about their campaigns with wild exaggeration. They are brash and loud, but an uneasy silence quickly falls when they see you approach. You notice that their hands are no longer grasping mugs of ale; they now rest upon the hilts of their heavy-bladed swords.

If you decide to offer to buy them a drink, turn to **30**.

If you wish to ask permission to join them, turn to **260**.

If you choose to ignore them, and would rather take a seat elsewhere and order some food, turn to **172**.

126

Arrows sweep across the river as the captain draws the company into line at the approach to the Tekaro bridge. The burnt-out hulks of siege towers and the bodies of dead soldiers lie strewn in heaps before the battered city gate. The fortified gatehouse bristles with archers, and the setting sun glints on the cauldrons of boiling oil and molten lead mounted on top of the battlements.

'Charge!' screams the captain and suddenly you are swept up and carried across the bridge by a frenzied wave of horsemen.

Thirty yards from the gate, the archers open fire.

Pick a number from the *Random Number Table*.

If the number you have picked is *0—3*, turn to **244**.
If the number you have picked is *4—6*, turn to **29**.
If the number you have picked is *7—9*, turn to **150**.

127 – *Illustration IX (overleaf)*

The door clicks shut behind you. It takes a few seconds for your eyes to grow accustomed to the dimly lit interior but the room appears to be the antechamber of a larger hall. Following the faint sound of voices, you pass through an archway, along a corridor and into the main hall. Gathered about a circular table of gleaming steel, a group of elderly men are poring over books, star charts and astral maps and engrossed in discussion. Globes of blue-white fire hang motionless in the air above them to illuminate their work. The old men do not see you until you are close to their steel table. Their reaction to your sudden appearance is astonishing – they look as though they have seen a ghost. There are yelps of shock and startled expressions; sweat forms on their brows. The sight is too much for one old man, who

IX. The elderly men are pouring over their books and star charts

swoons and faints, falling limply across his books and maps. Only one man remains calm and collected.

If you have ever visited a hut on Raider's Road in a previous Lone Wolf adventure, turn to **233**.
If you have never been to this place, turn to **6**.

128

Blood is pounding in your ears as you hear the approaching Yawshath splashing through the ankle-deep slime of the passage floor. Hideous laughter echoes from all sides, building up in a deafening crescendo. Suddenly, you realize the awful truth – there are in fact two Yawshaths. You have unwittingly entered their lair and now they have you trapped. You fight valiantly, but in the dark and fetid confines of the Yawshaths' den, the creatures overwhelm you and tear you to pieces.

Your quest and your life end here.

129

Suddenly, all hell breaks loose. Alarm bells ring, gruff voices bellow and scream and the crunching of boots on stone echoes round the town. A troop of soldiers surround you, their faces twisted and unnatural in the glare of their flaming torches. Your senses have been dulled by fatigue and you are dragged from the saddle and disarmed before you have had a chance to react. Cold iron chains are wound tightly around your arms and body and you are roughly pushed into a grey stone gaol. A wave of terror engulfs you as you catch a fleeting glimpse of a poster pasted to the gaol door. You see your own face before you; beneath it is written: 'Death sentence – by order of Lord Roark, Highborn of Amory.'

Within the hour, your head is resting upon the executioner's block. As the razor-sharp blade of a two-handed axe whistles towards your neck, the last sound you hear is the malicious and vengeful laugh of the young lordling.

Your life and your quest end here.

130

When they realize who you are, their suspicion vanishes to be replaced by respect; your reputation, it seems, has spread far beyond the borders of your northern home. Eagerly, the three men offer you a seat and call for a fresh round of ales at their expense. They are clearly honoured by your company and keen to press you about your exploits. You try to answer their barrage of questions with polite caution, taking care not to reveal the precise nature of your quest. However, despite their surly features and rough manner, you sense that these men are genuinely friendly.

Turn to **230**.

131

Your keen eyesight enables you to make out a line of dark shapes in front of the ship. It is a line of logs chained together: a boom lying directly in the path of the riverboat. Instantly you recognize the danger and rush to the bridge to warn the helmsman.

'Look out! There's a boom across the river!'

Desperately, he spins the ship's wheel but it is too late to avoid a collision. The screech of twisted metal and splintering wood tears through the silence as the *Kazonara* swings broadside-on into the chained logs. You brace yourself and hang on tightly as the boat lurches and rocks back and forth.

Turn to **224**.

132

You recognize the small flat-faced man: he was the umpire of the archery tournament. He asks you what is troubling you and you explain your sorry predicament.

'I'm sure we can find a solution to your problem,' he says, obviously relishing the thought of profiting by your misfortune. He will accept *either* 2 Special Items *or* 20 Gold Crowns in exchange for his horse.

If you agree to his proposal, turn to **212**.

If you cannot, or do not wish to, agree to his proposal, turn to **176**.

133

'You're looking at the "Hell-hole",' says an Ogron. 'When the siege began, Prince Ewevin sent ten humans in there to find out where it leads. When they never came back he sent ten Ogrons in. Ain't seen none of 'em since!'

Another Ogron, who is splitting a log with his bare hands, overhears the conversation. 'We've heard noises in the "Hell-hole" late at night,' he says guilefully, 'horrible noises.' He draws a fat finger across his blue-black throat before returning to his work.

If you wish to ask the Ogrons if you can use one of their pontoons to row across to the 'Hell-hole', turn to **179**.

If you decide to swim across instead, turn to **171**.

134

Beyond the Taunor valley, the highway twists and climbs across wooded hillsides, often plunging into narrow valleys where bubbling, trout-laden streams wend their way southwards to the Quarl. Butterflies gather in clouds above clumps of sweet-smelling flowers bordering the road, and the constant twitterings of birdsong add a sense of tranquillity to the beautiful countryside.

'It comforts me to know there is still one part of Lyris where war and death are unfamiliar visitors,' says Cyrilus, puffing nonchalantly on a long-stemmed clay pipe. 'Alas, nowadays, such peace is rare.'

The highway passes the ruins of a monastery and then descends steeply towards some log huts, clustered in a semi-circle at the approach to a stone bridge. A tall gate, flanked by two mighty towers of stone, commands the access to the bridge.

'The Denka Gate,' says Cyrilus, 'The toll is 3 Gold Crowns to cross the bridge, unless, of course, the gatekeeper is your brother.' He gives a sly wink and smiles. 'This may take a while – I haven't seen my brother Esmond for over a month and he is bound to want to hear all the latest gossip from Quarlen before he lets us cross.'

Cyrilus points out two of the log huts where wooden signs, carved in the shapes of an ale tankard and a loaf of bread, hang above the doors. 'The best ale and bread in all of Lyris. Mention my name and you'll be treated like a king.'

You are feeling hungry and thirsty after your long ride, and the prospect of free refreshment is very tempting.

If you wish to enter the ale hut, turn to **185**.
If you wish to enter the bread hut, turn to **287**.
If you decide to stay with Cyrilus and approach the Denka Gate, turn to **89**.

135

You ride between ranks of carved stone idols, whose mouths hold flickering torches, which illuminate this broad avenue. Mercenaries of all races and nationalities pack the street, talking, boasting or simply dozing in the shadows. At the end of the street, you arrive at a junction where a woman in filthy clothes sits nursing a crying child. As you pass she holds out a grimy hand and begs for Gold Crowns to feed her hungry baby.

If you wish to stop and give the poor woman some Gold Crowns, turn to **333**.
If you wish to ignore her and continue along the street, turn to **279**.

136

Your skill makes you sensitive to the faint aroma of gallowbrush. It is commonly known as 'Sleeptooth' in Sommerlund, for its crushed thorns make a powerful sleeping potion. You realize that, for reasons unknown to you, this man is trying to render you unconscious.

If you wish to draw your weapon and attack him, turn to **66**.

If you wish to put down your goblet and hurry out of the taxidermy, turn to **279**.

137

A peasant wagon and a merchant caravan bearing the toa-tree emblem of Casiorn are waiting in front of the town gate. You bring your horse to a halt and wait in line as the great door of rust-red iron slowly creaks open. A guard appears and gestures to the wagon and caravan to enter, but he lowers his spear menacingly as you prepare to follow. 'The town levy is 3 Gold Crowns, stranger. Pay or turn away.'

If you wish to pay the levy, give the guard 3 Gold Crowns and turn to **332**.

If you do not wish to pay the tax and wish to try to ride past the guard, turn to **115**.

138

No sooner have the doors of the inn slammed shut than you find yourself face to face with the city watch patrol. Every night, as a matter of routine, they wait for the drunks and rejects from the Inn of the Crossed Swords to be thrown on to the street. The burly guards grab you by the shoulders and attempt to strip you of your belongings before bundling you into a waiting cart. Instictively, you fight to break free but the guards take this as a threat. They unsheathe their swords and attack. You cannot evade combat and must fight the city watch to the death.

Varetta City Watch:
COMBAT SKILL 18   ENDURANCE 35

If you win the combat, turn to **34**.

139

You prise open the visor of the dead warrior's helmet, half-expecting to see the rough features of a bandit or highwayman. It comes as a shock to find the cold and empty eyes of a dead woman staring back at you. The shape of her body was concealed by the thick plates of armour and a clutch of magras reeds in the mouthpiece of her visor had effectively disguised her voice.

You find few clues to identify her: an axe, a pouch containing 11 Gold Crowns, a Dagger and a Silver Brooch are all she carries: hired killers travel light. You examine the Silver Brooch and decide to keep it. (Mark this as a Special Item on your *Action Chart*.) There is something vaguely familiar about her face but you cannot remember why. Suddenly, your thoughts return to the plight of your companion – his life is in danger. You mount your horse without further delay and gallop across the Denka Bridge in pursuit.

Turn to **39**.

140

You press on diligently, counting the steps that take you along the sewer until you reach a narrow vault a little over one hundred and fifty yards from the previous junction. An iron ladder, its rungs pitted with rust, rises out of the water to an arched stone door. Beneath the door, the sewer continues into the darkness.

If you wish to climb the ladder and investigate the arched door, turn to **259**.

If you wish to continue along the passage, turn to **339**.

141

Cyrilus offers to stay and look after the horses while you take part in the contest. He says that archery holds no interest for him, but you suspect this is just an excuse to take an afternoon nap. You hand him the reins of your horse and hurry to join a line of men waiting to enter the tournament field.

The event reminds you of a Sommlending village pageant and the jugglers, the dancers and the numerous sideshows all add to the festive spirit. Eventually, you reach the gate where a cheerful old lady is collecting the 2 Gold Crowns entrance fee. You hand over your Crowns (remember to mark these off on your *Action Chart*), and enter a large tent where the other competitors are stringing their bows.

If you have a bow, turn to **340**.
If you do not have a bow, turn to **18**.

142

The blade whistles towards your chest. You throw yourself to the deck – but are your reactions fast enough to save you from this deadly blade?

Pick a number from the *Random Number Table*. If you have the Magnakai Discipline of Nexus or Divination, deduct 2 from the number you have picked. If you possess a shield, deduct 3 from the number you have picked.

If your total is now 4 or less, turn to **184**.
If it is now 5 or more, turn to **51**.

143

You have ridden less than a mile when the surface of the highway changes from cobblestones to flattened earth. There are no fresh tracks in this earth, so the riders cannot have left the village by this road.

If you wish to ride back to the village, turn to **52**.

If you wish to hide in the trees bordering the highway to wait and see if the riders show themselves, turn to **196**.

If you wish to return to the junction and take the hill track, turn to **241**.

144

The dormitory is a long, narrow, low-ceilinged hall at the rear of the tavern, full of snoring mercenaries and the smell of stale sweat. You pick a straw mattress next to a window, braving the cold draught whipping through its shattered pane; at least this carries away the foul air.

In the middle of the night you are woken by a bright light. A shooting star of sun-like brilliance arcs over the city, shedding a rainbow of colour over the drab dormitory. You watch as the star slowly disappears before settling down once more to your much-needed rest. It seems as if you have only just closed your eyes when the loud and loathsome clang of the dormitory bell fills your ears.

'All awake! All awake! A new day dawns, my fine brave lads!' The voice of the tavern-keeper is echoed by the groans of a hundred bleary-eyed soldiers, as they drag themselves coughing and wheezing from their beds.

You dress, gather your equipment and collect your horse from the stable. However, it is not until you are studying the route to Brass Street that you discover that an item is missing from your Backpack; it was stolen during the night. Erase one Backpack Item of your choice from your *Action Chart* before setting off for Brass Street.

Turn to **300**.

The survivors flee into the dark, leaving their leader and over half their number lying dead at your feet. Leaning down from the saddle, you snatch a pouch that hangs from the dead leader's belt. It contains 12 Gold Crowns and a Ruby Ring. You may keep the Crowns and the Ring. If you take the Ring, mark it on your *Action Chart* as a Special Item which is to be carried in your pocket.

You hear the crunch of boots on stone as a group of soldiers tramp up the street from the river, moving disdainfully through the crowds of people that have gathered to watch. Sheathing your blood-smeared weapon, you rein your horse about to take off along the darkening street.

Turn to **289**.

By noon, the hills lie far behind and you catch your first sight of the snow-capped Ceners. To the south, nestling at the foot of this mountain range, is Amory. You are tired after your ride but you know you must press on if you are to reach the town by nightfall. You reach a junction where a stone signpost indicates two directions: north-west to Soren and south to Amory. Both towns lie exactly 25 miles from this point. You are hungry and must now eat a Meal or lose 3 ENDURANCE points.

If you wish to continue your ride to Amory, turn to **96**.

If you wish to change direction and head for Soren, turn to **247**.

147

The street is narrow and crowded with all manner of fighting men: mercenaries from the south who have come to Varetta in search of employment. They fill the tiny alleyways that branch off from the main street and the air is full with their noisy banter. The smell of food mingles with the odour of sweat and leather, and flickering lanterns swing in the chill night breeze. Nobody pays attention to you and you follow the winding cobblestones without any hindrance until you reach a magnificent half-timbered building. Large bow windows display an eye-catching assortment of creatures of all shapes and sizes, stuffed or mounted on wooden plaques. A sign by the door reads:

CHANDA – TAXIDERMIST

If you wish to dismount and enter this fascinating shop, turn to **121**.

If you wish to continue along the winding street, turn to **279**.

148

'If you will not part with the bow, then perhaps you have something else of value that will persuade me to part with my horse?' he says, shrewdly.

Altan will accept either 2 Special Items, or 20 Gold Crowns in exchange for his horse.

If you agree to his proposal, turn to **212**.

If you cannot, or do not wish to, agree to his proposal, turn to **176**.

149

'May I offer you some refreshment before you leave? I can see by the dust on your tunic that you have travelled far today.' The man brings forward a silver tray on which stands a ruby glass decanter and two crystal goblets. He fills the goblets with wine and offers one to you.

If you wish to accept his generous offer, take the goblet and turn to **228**.

If you wish to decline his offer and leave the taxidermy, turn to **279**.

150

Your horse is hit and mortally wounded. It stumbles, and in the shrieking press of horses and men, you are barged aside and thrown over the stone parapet of the bridge. You hit the water head first and are swept away by the powerful current of the River Quarl.

Turn to **306**.

151 – *Illustration X*

The narrow street begins its steep descent towards the wharves and huge warehouses that line the River Quarl. The sun is now below the horizon and lanterns are being lit in the twisting alleys and passages of the dingy town. From open alehouse doors the red glare of roaring fires colours the oily black cobblestones.

X.   'Are you a believer or an unbeliever?'

You have been riding for barely a minute when the street ahead is blocked by a procession of men, advancing up the hill towards you. They are dressed in red cloaks with black hoods and carry large scarlet candles, which flicker in the chill evening breeze.

Their leader is a tall man with hard grey eyes. He fixes you with a stare and slowly raises his hands; the procession halts. 'Are you a believer or an unbeliever?' he cries, his voice as piercing as his stare.

If you wish to answer 'believer', turn to **108**.

If you wish to answer 'unbeliever', turn to **67**.

If you have ever been to the buried temple of Maaken, turn to **294**.

152

You agree to meet the captain in the apothecary in one hour's time before beginning your exploration of Luyen. Further along the street you notice a dusty shop window full of weapons. Above the door you see a sign.

DEMICO'S WEAPONSHOP

All Weapons Bought & Sold

If you wish to enter this second-hand weapons shop, turn to **98**.

If you would rather continue along the street, turn to **275**.

153

The bolt screams through the air and hits you from the side, tearing a furrow of skin and muscle from your ribs before embedding itself in the side of the log hut. (You lose 5 ENDURANCE points.) Stifling a cry of

pain, you stagger towards your horse. The w
has discarded his empty crossbow and is
spurring his mount across the bridge in pursuit of his
companions.

If you have a bow, turn to **178**.
If you do not have a bow and have to mount your
horse and give chase, turn to **39**.

154

The man grasps the woman by the wrist and
uncovers the arm cradled around her baby. Clasped
between her fingers is a hat pin with which she pricks
the baby's skin to make it cry.

'You'll be beggin' in the streets yourself before dawn
if you be taken in b'likes of her,' he says.

The woman pulls free from his grasp, curses, and
disappears among the scruffy crowd of mercenaries
wandering the street.

'Who d'you serve?' asks the man, his brutal face
framed by a closely cropped red beard, 'or d'you
come in search of a captain, eh?'

If you wish to talk to this man, turn to **181**.
If you wish to ignore him and ride off, turn to **279**.

155

You release the arrow but it narrowly misses its target
and clatters harmlessly against the chapel wall. The
creature is now upon you and there is no time to draw
another weapon.

Yawshath: COMBAT SKILL 22   ENDURANCE 38

You must fight the first round of combat with your bare hands (deduct 4 points from your COMBAT SKILL for this round only). At the start of the second round, you may draw a weapon (if you have one), and fight the creature normally. If you survive 4 rounds of combat, you can evade the Yawshath by escaping through the archway by which you entered the chapel.

If you survive 4 rounds of combat and wish to evade, turn to **305**.

If you win the combat, turn to **112**.

156

Only brute force will break the seal of encrusted filth and open the door.

Sewer Door:
COMBAT SKILL 13   ENDURANCE (Resistance) 35

To break open the door, you should follow the normal combat rules. Any ENDURANCE points that you lose during this 'combat' represent the fatigue you suffer as you hack and batter the door.

If you wish to cease 'combat' at any time and continue along the sewer, turn to **339**.

If you reduce the door's resistance (ENDURANCE) to 0, turn to **200**.

157

The food tastes even better than it smells (restore 1 ENDURANCE point). If you wish, you may also take enough bread for up to 2 Meals. Remember to make the necessary adjustment to your *Action Chart*.

You are about to walk around the counter to examine the back room when you hear a faint cry for help. It is Cyrilus – he is in trouble.

Turn to **317**.

158

The passage leads to a vaulted cellar, as cold and as silent as a tomb. Gwynian talks with his brothers who then hurry off towards a distant portal. As they disappear into the dark, he returns to your side, his face sombre but composed.

'The Lorestone of Varetta is hidden in the crypt of the cathedral of Tekaro. This key will unlock the tomb in which it lies.' He produces a Silver Key from his sleeve and gives it to you.

'My brothers will provide a swift horse for your journey. When the observatory clock strikes midnight, enter the portal and follow the passage to the end. It passes beneath the city wall and your horse will be waiting where the passage comes to the surface. You are welcome to take any Items you require from this cellar that may be of use to you on your quest. May the gods protect you, Lone Wolf.' You nod your thanks and watch as Gwynian disappears into the portal.

The cellar is well stocked with provisions and you find the following Items that could be of use on your journey to Tekaro:

> Quarterstaff
> Enough food for 3 Meals
> Mace
> Brass Whistle
> Rope
> Short Sword

Together with the Silver Key that Gwynian gave you (mark this as a Special Item that you keep in your pocket), you collect together all the Items you wish to keep and settle down for the long wait till midnight.

Turn to **175**.

159

'You insult us, stranger,' hisses the scar-faced man as he springs to his feet. Suddenly, the noisy hall becomes as silent as the grave: all eyes are on you. Some merchants to your left hurriedly move away as the two other warriors kick over their table and draw their swords.

'Strike!' they shout and attack. You must fight all three as one enemy. You cannot evade combat or make use of a bow.

Varetian Mercenaries:
COMBAT SKILL 26   ENDURANCE 35

If you win the combat, turn to **48**.

160

Grabbing hold of the door, you slam it shut as hard as you can. The youth is unprepared and the door catches him squarely in the face, somersaulting him backwards over a table and chair. As the door rebounds open again you see him sprawled flat on his back, unconscious, with a huge lump beginning to swell in the centre of his forehead.

You pick up a square of blue card and notice that it is stamped with today's date. This will grant you access to the town of Amory, but only for today. You pocket the Cess (mark this as a Special Item on your *Action Chart*) and leave before the youth comes to his senses.

Turn to **146**.

161

As you drop your belt pouch into the palm of the robber, you feel an agonizing pain tear through your side.

'Did you think we would let you live to identify us?' sneers the robber, but his voice fades as you collapse to the floor. The robbers melt away into the crowd and by the time your murder has been discovered, they are safely hiding in another part of the vast city.

Your life and your quest end here.

162

Instinctively, you dive and roll, drawing your weapon as you rise again to your feet. Your lightning-fast reactions have saved you from the clutches of a shambling, blunt-nosed monster that preys on unwary pilgrims to this spa. However, it is not deterred and with a hideous snickering caw, its feral eyes glowing with hatred, it shuffles hungrily towards you.

If you have a bow, turn to **198**.
If you do not have a bow, turn to **343**.

163

Twenty yards out from the bank you hear a cry go up: 'Stop that man!' The Ogrons drop their tools and scurry to the water's edge. Some of them have bows which they hurriedly load and fire.

Pick a number from the *Random Number Table*. If you have the Magnakai Discipline of Invisibility, add 4 to the number you have picked.

If your total score is now 3 or less, turn to **197**.
If it is 4 or higher, turn to **229**.

164 *— Illustration XI*

Your Magnakai skill makes you particularly alert to the deadly missile screaming towards your chest – suddenly everything seems to be happening in slow motion. You pull away from the bolt just in time and the quarrel merely grazes your shoulder. (You lose 2 ENDURANCE points.) You see your attacker hurl the crossbow to the ground. From within the closed helmet of black steel a voice shouts out: 'Die north-lander!'

The warrior charges out of the Denka Gate with an axe held high in his hand. You cannot avoid him and must fight him to the death.

Armoured Assassin:
COMBAT SKILL 24   ENDURANCE 26

XI.   From within the closed helm of black steel a voice shouts out
'Die northlander!'

Due to the speed of this attack, you cannot make use of a bow. However, if you have the Magnakai Discipline of Animal Control, you may add 1 point to your COMBAT SKILL for the duration of this fight.

If you win the fight, turn to **28**.

165

'Certainly, sir. We of the guild of city criers are only too pleased to be of service,' says the Kloon, waddling over to the bookshelves. He scampers to the top and removes a slim map from between a stack of papers before scuttling back down and depositing it at your feet.

'That will be 5 Gold Crowns, sir,' he says, in a firm but polite tone.

If you wish to pay the Kloon for the Map of Varetta, turn to **16**.

If you cannot or do not wish to pay him, turn to **262**.

166

Valiantly your horse attempts to clear the high-sided wagon but the long day's ride has taken its toll. Suddenly you are thrown forward in the saddle as its forelegs crash against the wagon's rail. You cling desperately to the reins as your terrified horse scatters the cargo and then lands with a tremendous crash on the cobblestoned street. You manage to regain control and spur her along the winding street that leads away from the square. Only when the curses of the town guard can no longer be heard do you rein in your terrified and exhausted mare and take stock of her injuries. The forelegs are bruised but the skin is not broken. With a good night's rest she should be perfectly all right by morning.

As you remount, you discover to your dismay that the flap of your Backpack is unbuckled. A quick check reveals that two items are missing, which fell from your pack during the jump. Erase any two Backpack Items from your *Action Chart*.

Turn to **332**.

167

Loud and raucous laughter greets your tired ears as you enter the Stornside Tavern. A motley throng of drinkers, over-dressed and over-armed, prop up the bar along the back wall. Suddenly a voice calls out to you and you raise your weary eyes. It is the captain, the mercenary leader you met at the Inn of the Crossed Swords.

'Well met, my friend,' he cries and slaps you enthusiastically on the shoulder. 'So you've changed your mind. You have come to join my band of fearless fighters.' Before you have a chance to reply, a foaming tankard is thrust into your hand.

'To the battle and a full purse!' he shouts, and his toast is echoed by a score of drunken voices.

The captain and his men are bound for Eula aboard the riverboat that leaves at midnight. If you sail with them he will pay for your passage.

If you wish to sail with the captain at midnight, turn to **341**.

If you wish to make your own way to Tekaro by road, turn to **118**.

168

It is nearly dark when you catch sight of a tavern on the road ahead. Two guttering torches set into rusty brackets illuminate the sign nailed above the door:

THE HALFWAY INN

You recognize the name of the tavern that Cyrilus spoke of this morning, and it grieves you that he is not here to accompany you. Distant thunder rumbles through the hills as you stable your horse and enter the welcoming warmth of the taproom. The tavern is alive with the chatter of merchants, the clink of glasses and the crackle of a blazing fire. The centre of the room is dominated by a small stage on which a conjurer is performing his tricks to the delight of the customers.

If you wish to stand and watch the conjurer, turn to **199**.

If you wish to enquire about a room for the night, turn to **253**.

169

The iron door is unlocked but you discover to your horror that the hinges are so badly rusted that the door will not move an inch. Suddenly, the Yawshath appears at the top of the stone staircase, snickering and gibbering horribly. It fixes you with its red eyes and prepares to pounce.

If you have completed the Lore-circle of Fire (that is, you possess the Magnakai Disciplines of Weaponmastery and Huntmastery), turn to **65**.

If you do not possess these skills and wish to prepare to defend yourself, turn to **222**.

If you would rather turn and run deeper into the ruins, turn to **285**.

170

The riverboat is still rocking violently from the collision, throwing you off balance. You raise an arrow, take aim at the man's chest and try to anticipate the shift of the deck as you prepare to fire.

Pick a number from the *Random Number Table*. If you have the Magnakai Discipline of Weaponmastery with a bow, add 3 to your score. If you have the Magnakai Discipline of Huntmastery, add 1 to your score.

If your total is now 5 or lower, turn to **23**.
If it is now 6 or higher, turn to **265**.

171

The water is freezing cold. It saps your strength and you find it increasingly harder to swim against the strong converging river currents. Eventually, you reach the rocky bank and stagger ashore near the sewer outfall. Unless you have the Magnakai Discipline of Nexus, you lose 1 ENDURANCE point due to the cold.

Turn to **249**.

172

You choose a seat near the corner: one that is laid for dinner and offers a clear view of the hall. A serving girl soon appears carrying a platter laden with roasted meat, and she proceeds to stack a generous helping on your plate.

'Two Gold Crowns, if you please, sir,' she says, presenting an open hand bloodied by the food.

You pay (remember to deduct the Crowns from your *Action Chart*) and settle down to your feast. While you are eating, you are approached by the innkeeper. He is a fat, oily individual with small, piggish eyes.

'My lad tells me that he's tended to your mare – she's in good 'ands 'ere – the best stables in all o' Quarlen.' The man shifts nervously from one foot to the other, as if he is uncomfortable in your presence. 'You'll be wantin' a room I take it?'

You finish a mouthful of food before nodding your reply. 'You're in luck, my friend,' he answers, obviously relieved that you have turned out to be a paying guest. 'We 'ave one room left – Room 17.'

He produces a plain iron key from his apron pocket and sets it down beside your plate. 'That'll be 3 Gold

Crowns, sir – in advance.' You pay the innkeeper, and slip the key into your pocket.

Turn to **219**.

173

You notice that the man's clothes and hair are streaked with blood. Your initial instinct is to use your Magnakai skill to heal his wounds but as he reaches the church gate you suddenly realize that he is not wounded at all. The red stains are berry juice; his injuries are fake.

If you wish to challenge him, turn to **337**.

If you wish to gallop away from the church as quickly as possible, turn to **191**.

174

A cry of pained surprise escapes from between your clenched teeth as the bolt tears both the skin and muscle from your ribs (lose 5 ENDURANCE points). However, your sheer strength of will, heightened by your Kai training and discipline, helps you to overcome the shock of impact and remain upright in the saddle.

If you are still alive after this attack, turn to **234**.

175

When the observatory clock strikes twelve, you are poised and ready to enter the portal. You follow a dry stone passageway until you arrive at an iron door. It opens with a grating squeal and a gust of damp, earthy air, mixed with a strange sweetness, billows out. Before you, a narrow stone stairway twists away into the darkness. You are forced to tread carefully on the green and slippery steps. At the bottom of the stairs a rough-hewn tunnel disappears to the west. You press on and eventually arrive at another iron door. Gwynian has kept his word, for beyond the door awaits a fine liver chestnut mare, saddled and ready to ride.

You are in a small copse close to a highway junction. In the light of the moon you can see a signpost that indicates two destinations – Amory and Soren. Consult the map at the front of this book before deciding which way to go.

If you decide to take the highway to Amory, turn to **331**.

If you decide to take the highway to Soren, turn to **267**.

176

You decline the offer and go in search of some other means of finding Cyrilus. The village stables are locked and guarded, but at the rear of the blacksmithy you discover just what you are looking for. A young stallion is pacing the paddock, its saddle and blanket slung over the gate. At first he is wary of your approach, but he soon senses that you mean no harm and you have no difficulty in preparing him for the ride. Once clear of the paddock, you canter around the blacksmithy and on to the highway.

Turn to **271**.

177

'Ah! You're in luck, stranger. The dice favour you tonight.' The man staggers drunkenly to his feet and points to an alley in the middle distance where a doorway is just visible in the shadows. 'The city criers live there. They'll tell you the way to Brass Street.'

You nod your thanks and spur your horse along the street towards the darkened doorway.

Turn to **25**.

178

The warrior gallops off, his cloak billowing from his shoulders like huge black wings as his horse speeds across the bridge. You draw an arrow to your lips and take careful aim – you will have no second chance.

Pick a number from the *Random Number Table*. If you have the Magnakai Discipline of Weaponmastery with a bow, add 3 to the number you have picked.

If your total score is now 7 or below, turn to **296**.
If your total score is now *8* or above, turn to **303**.

179

They will not let you touch any of the pontoons. If any go missing they will each receive 100 lashes as punishment for their negligence. They keep a watchful eye on you until you leave the camp. As it is now impossible to take one of the pontoons, you resign yourself to a long cold swim.

Turn to **171**.

180

Trembling with pain and fury, the wounded lordling staggers back towards the door. 'I shall have your life for this – mark my words,' he cries.

The mocking cheers of the crowd echo in his wake as he turns and disappears into the night.

Turn to **281**.

181

You learn that the man's name is Redbeard and that he hails from Soren, a town to the west of Varetta. He is sergeant-at-arms to a captain of mercenaries and has recently returned from battle against the Magadorians. He offers to take you to meet his captain who, he says, is the best soldier he has ever had the good fortune to serve under.

If you wish to accept his offer, turn to **256**.
If you decide to decline his offer, bid him farewell and continue along the street, turn to **279**.

182

You duck and weave as you race through the undergrowth. A charge of crackling power strikes a branch above your head; it narrowly misses you as it falls in a blazing heap by your side. You sidestep in time to avoid another charge which tears a hole in a tree trunk large enough to rest your head. You reach your horse and take off along the highway at a gallop, thankful to be alive. You have witnessed a secret ritual of the Cener Druids and survived the encounter – few can boast as much!

Turn to **102**.

183

A loud cheer shatters the silence as Altan's winning arrow hits the target. The villagers are thrilled to have witnessed such an exciting tournament and surge across the field, eager to offer Altan their praise and congratulations. As the tall woodsman disappears from view amid the teeming crowd, you take the opportunity to slip away unnoticed.

If you have used a borrowed bow for the tournament, you must return it to the tent before making your way back to Cyrilus.

Turn to **33**.

184

The dagger shaves a lock of hair from your head before sinking inches deep into the wooden parapet rail. The shock of your swift move unnerves the pirate and he is off balance when you leap to your feet and attack. Before he knows what has hit him, he is tumbling over the side into the cold deep waters of the Storn.

Turn to **254**.

185

Having hitched your horse to a rail, you climb the crooked steps leading to the door of the ale hut. Cyrilus is announcing his arrival by rapping on the Denka Gate with his staff and shouting for his brother to open up. You smile at his growing impatience as he hammers at the gate; if his brother is anything like Cyrilus, he is probably fast asleep.

Inside, the hut looks deserted, but as you approach the bar you find a man slouched on a low stool, half-asleep with a tankard in his hand.

If you wish to wake him, turn to **93**.

If you wish to draw some ale from a cask on the bar, turn to **266**.

186

You concentrate your Magnakai Discipline on agitating the particles of dirt that wedge the door shut. Gradually the stone begins to vibrate and cracks appear around the jamb as the dirt begins to crumble.

Turn to **200**.

187

Twisting aside at the last moment, you manage to avoid one deadly pikehead but cannot dodge the other. It rips into your tunic and scrapes your flesh (lose 3 ENDURANCE points). Your anger rises and you fight to free your weapon, which has become entangled in the straps of your saddle. The guards see that you are trapped and push forward before you have a chance to retaliate.

Turn to **22**.

Your immediate peril stops you dwelling too much on the reason why these riders should try to abduct Cyrilus. However, it does occur to you that he is neither wealthy nor powerful and so a poor prospect for a rich ransom.

As you reach the bottom of the wooded crag, a stone church and graveyard loom into view at a point where the highway turns sharply to the west. Blocking the road, on a charger as black as midnight, sits a scar-faced young man. His eyes, set in a white and disfigured face, burn with a cold dark glow. You recognize him immediately. It is Roark, the lordling you defeated at the Barrel Bridge Tavern.

If you possess a Silver Brooch, turn to **31**.
If you do not have this Special Item, turn to **14**.

189

The thin-faced merchant bids you sit at his table, his shrewd eyes narrowing at the thought of a new and profitable deal. You tell him that you require some information and may be willing to pay for it if the price is right. He asks the nature of this information, but when you ask for the directions to Brass Street, his business-like mood suddenly changes.

Turn to **47**.

190

Crazed with hatred and rage, the Yawshath springs from the top of the mound of rubble and dives straight for you. Its frenzy has made it blind to the peril

XII. On a charger as black as midnight sits a scar-faced young man

of the precipice and, as you leap aside, it hurtles past and disappears into the void. Seconds later you hear a shriek as it crashes into the rocks hundreds of feet below.

Shaken, but thankful to be alive, you return to the chapel and fill your glass jar with Taunor Water (there is enough spa water to restore 6 ENDURANCE points). You may drink the Water now or place it in your Backpack for future use.

If you wish to make a search of the chapel, turn to **24**.

If you decide to return to Cyrilus, turn to **338**.

191

You are tired after your long night's ride but you know you must press on if you are to reach the town of Soren by nightfall. You come to a shallow stream, which crosses the highway, and here you stop briefly at a ford to wash and rest. You must also now eat a Meal or lose 3 ENDURANCE points. Beside the ford stands a signpost pointing to the west:

SOREN – 25 MILES

Turn to **102**.

192

Splashing through ankle-deep slime, you suddenly catch sight of two glowing pinpoints of red light in the darkness ahead. They grow larger and brighter and suddenly you realize the awful truth – there are two Yawshaths. Their hideous laughter builds to a deafening climax as they close in for the kill. Unwittingly, you have entered their lair and now they have you trapped.

You fight valiantly but the creatures finally overwhelm you in the dark and fetid confines of the passage. You are torn limb from limb, with no one to hear your cries for help.

Your quest and your life end here in the dungeons of Castle Taunor.

193

The Kloon begins to wail as you dispatch his vicious watchdog. With scarlet tears streaming from his crimson eyes, he scampers out of the room and bolts the door. After wiping the blood from your hands, you pick up the Map of Varetta and hurry out of the room.

Turn to **16**.

194

The howling mob scream like men possessed as they hack and slash at your unarmoured legs. If you have the Magnakai Discipline of Animal Control, you may add 2 to your COMBAT SKILL for the duration of this fight, for it enables you to command your horse to attack with its hooves.

Acolytes of Vashna:
COMBAT SKILL 22   ENDURANCE 48

If you wish to evade combat at any time, turn to **289**.

If you win the combat, turn to **145**.

195

Suddenly, you sense that you are in grave peril and you listen carefully at the keyhole to determine what is being said by the preacher.

'. . . and so I beseech you, my brothers, do not listen to Gwynian's foolish and dangerous theory. The star that shone in the night is a warning to us to guard our knowledge, to keep safe the secret of the Lorestone. We must stop all those who would use its power for their own wicked ends.'

The preacher's words are answered by loud chanting: 'Keep the secret, keep the secret, keep the secret!'

The sound of a key in the lock makes you start. The meeting has come to an end and the congregation are preparing to leave. Quickly, you sprint away and take cover in a darkened doorway. The brown-robed men pour out of the temple and disperse, but a small group are heading towards your hiding place; if you stay where you are you will be seen for sure. Without a second thought, you push open the door and enter.

Turn to **127**.

196

It is only a matter of minutes before the riders appear. They ride in single file with the unconscious wizard in tow behind the last man's horse.

If you have a bow and want to ambush them as they ride past your hiding place, turn to **20**.

If you wish to attack the last rider and try to recapture Cyrilus, turn to **203**.

If you wish to let them pass and then follow them, turn to **227**.

197

You are almost out of bowshot when an arrow gashes your calf (lose 2 ENDURANCE points), and thuds into the side of the pontoon. You bite your lip and stifle your urge to scream, for you are now within range of the city's archers. As soon as the pontoon grounds on the bank, you slip ashore and creep across the rocks towards the sewer outfall.

Turn to **249**.

198

There is only enough time for you to fire one shot before the monster is upon you; you cannot afford to miss. To stop the creature dead in its tracks, you need to hit a vital organ, but in the gloom of this ruined chapel it is difficult to see your target clearly.

If you wish to take aim at the creature's eyes, turn to **268**.

If you wish to take aim at its heart, turn to **243**.

If you wish to take aim at its legs, turn to **95**.

199

Having removed a bunch of flowers from the ear of a startled merchant and a clucking hen from the petti-coat of the merchant's wife, the flamboyantly dressed conjurer calls for silence from his cheering audience before announcing his next trick. Two children shuffle on to the stage, their bodies and faces completely hidden by long black gowns that are tied at their foreheads. Only their hair, blond and black is visible.

'I'm a boy,' says the one with black hair.
'I'm a girl,' says the one with blond hair, the voice identical to the first.

The conjurer steps forward and says that they are a boy and a girl but at least one of them is lying. He asks which is which and invites the audience to bet on the answer.

If you wish to bet on this conundrum, turn to **245**.
If you do not wish to gamble and would rather approach the bar and enquire about a room for the night, turn to **253**.

200

The old stone door creaks slowly open and, as the dust settles, you find yourself staring into the crypt of Tekaro Cathedral. Stepping into the chill stale air, your heart begins to pound in your chest; the Lorestone is here – you can feel it.

Beams of ashen moonlight filter into the crypt, illuminating a line of sombre granite tombs that lie like sleeping giants under the earth. Clutching the Silver Key, you examine them one by one for the lock that guards the legendary Lorestone.

You find the lock and insert the key but you are suddenly distracted, on the brink of discovery, by the creature that is advancing through the sewer door.

Turn to **334**.

201

The sergeant orders his men to stand back – he is confident that he can defeat you unaided and is eager to show off his fighting prowess. A smile of expectant triumph curls his scarred lips as he raises his spear and shield. You may fight this combat with any weapon except a bow.

Town Sergeant: COMBAT SKILL 18   ENDURANCE 27

If you win and the combat lasts 3 rounds or less, turn to **15**.
If the combat lasts longer than 3 rounds, turn to **87**.

202

The room is small, shabby and bare except for the battered straw mattress and threadbare carpet covering the floor. You lock the door and settle down to sleep, using your Backpack as a pillow and your cloak as a blanket. In the middle of the night you are woken by a bright light. A shooting star of sun-like brilliance arcs over the city, shedding a rainbow of colour across your drab surroundings. You watch the star as it slowly disappears before settling down once more to your much-needed rest. It seems as if you have only just closed your eyes when the loud and loathsome clang of the tavern bell fills your ears.

'All awake, all awake! A new day dawns my fine brave lads!' As the voice of the tavern-keeper echoes through the inn, you dress, gather your equipment and then collect your horse from the stable.

Your rest restores 1 ENDURANCE point. Make the necessary change to your *Action Chart* before setting off on your search for Brass Street.

Turn to **300**.

203

With bated breath you wait for the enemy to pass. As the last man rides into view, you break cover and attack him with deadly efficiency. He tries to raise a shield to block your blow but cannot react in time to save his life. As he tumbles to the ground, you cut the reins from his saddle and take off along the highway with the unconscious wizard in tow.

Turn to **188**.

204

Prince Ewevin holds a conference of war. An hour passes before the captain returns to the company and his news is greeted with mixed feelings by his travel-weary men.

'We ride into battle tonight,' he says, his voice firm and unwavering. 'We are to lead an attack across the Tekaro Bridge to break the city gate, which is greatly weakened at the moment. We must attack tonight if the enemy are to be prevented from making good their repairs.'

Many of his men, battle-hardened veterans of countless wars, cannot hide their fear that the attack is suicidal. The gate is heavily defended by archers and cannot be taken without a great loss of life.

'Each man will be paid a thousand crowns,' says the captain, hoping to change their minds with the promise of gold, but few are impressed; what use is gold to them if they are killed in the assault? 'Those who wish to fight can stay by my side,' he bellows, his steel-blue eyes blazing with anger. 'Those who will not fight can go.'

If you wish to stay with the captain and assault the city gate, turn to **126**.
If you decide to leave, turn to **280**.

205

Your Huntmastery enables you to identify hidden weaknesses in both the Jakan and the Kalte bone bow. If you were to choose either of these weapons, your chances of success would be greatly reduced. Forewarned by your Magnakai skill, you make the best choice: the Durenese hunting bow.

Turn to **60**.

206

You sense that potential danger lies within the copse, and that the chanting is part of a sacrificial ceremony.

If you wish to investigate the ceremony, turn to **13**.
If you wish to avoid it and continue along the highway to Soren, turn to **102**.

207

With bated breath, you manouevre the noose around the head of the warhammer. It takes over five minutes to secure the rope and retrieve the weapon.

Close examination of your find reveals it to be a very fine weapon, wrought of a metal called bronin, which looks identical to newly cast bronze but, unlike regular alloys of copper and tin, will not tarnish with use or age.

If you wish to keep this Bronin Warhammer, mark it on your *Action Chart* as a Weapon. When you use it in combat it will add 1 point to your COMBAT SKILL total. Satisfied that nothing else of value has been overlooked, you leave the chapel and return to Cyrilus.

Turn to **338**.

208

Your Magnakai Discipline reveals the man's hiding place – he is crouching behind a worktable to your right. Suddenly, he jumps up and hurls a glass flask at your face but, forewarned by your Magnakai skill, you are prepared for this ambush. You duck and the flask whistles overhead to smash against the far wall. A bubbling hiss fills the air as the contents of the flask corrode and dissolve the plaster. With a flurry of vile curses, the man unsheathes a rapier and attacks.

Chanda the Taxidermist:
COMBAT SKILL 17   ENDURANCE 24

If you wish to evade combat at any time by running from the shop, mounting your horse and galloping away, turn to **279**.

If you win the combat, turn to **8**.

209

Trembling with fear, you draw the bowstring and fire. The arrow glances off its armoured head and shatters against the crypt wall. There is no time for a second shot. You discard your bow and prepare for close combat as the creature moves in to strike.

Turn to **344**.

210

Less than a mile from the village, the road descends into a narrow valley where a castle, part of which has fallen into ruin, is set on a rock shelf beneath a mossy precipice. 'Castle Taunor,' says Cyrilus, shielding his eyes from the glare of the afternoon sun. 'It's a place of pilgrimage for many people; the water from its spa

has great healing properties.' He leans forward,
removes a small glass jar from his saddlebag and
offers it to you. 'Taunor Water could be useful to a
warrior such as you.'

> If you wish to take the glass jar and collect some
> Taunor Water, turn to **63**.
> If you choose to decline Cyrilus' suggestion and
> continue your journey to Varetta, turn to **134**.

211

The captain is an imposing man, tall, muscular, with a
strong-jawed face, unmarked by battle or disease.
His blond hair is cropped close to his head and,
likewise, his beard and moustache are trimmed close
to his tanned skin. You are invited to join his
company and, as you drink your ale, you listen to
their proud talk of war, of victories, of loot and wages
– but never of defeat.

The captain and his men have grown tired of the war
in the north. Prince Janveal of Helin is close to ruin,
having sold all he owns to pay for a war against Baron
Maghao of Karkaste that he cannot hope to win. The
prince's troops are demoralized and his mercenaries
desert him at the first opportunity. You learn that the
captain is recruiting men for a campaign in the south.
The war between Salony and Slovia has reached
boiling point and there is much gold to be had in the
service of the Salonese Prince Ewevin while he
besieges the city of Tekaro.

'You have the mien of a skilful warrior,' says the
captain, his steel-blue eyes cold and unblinking.
'Why not join my company? I have need of fighters

and I pay with gold, not promises. We leave for Tekaro at dawn – will you ride with us?'

Politely you refuse the captain's offer, saying that you have come to Varetta on other business.

'What business is there for a warrior other than war?' retorts the captain, to the raucous delight of his men. You finish your ale and bid the captain and his company goodnight.

'If you change your mind, join us at Soren. We sail the river from there in two days' time.'

If you have a Map of Varetta, turn to **17**.
If you do not possess this Special Item, turn to **104**.

212

You keep your side of the bargain. (Remember to make the necessary adjustments to your *Action Chart*.) In exchange, he hands over the reins of his horse. 'Good luck, northlander,' he says, as you climb into the saddle. 'I hope you find your companion. He is a lucky man to have a friend such as you.'

You shout a farewell as you spur your new horse to the gallop.

Turn to **39**.

213

You follow the man through a curtained archway to a high-vaulted chamber that reeks with the pungent smell of preservatives and dead bodies. Several carcasses of exotic animals hang from hooks in the ceiling, and disected heads destined for trophy plaques are laid on the large workbenches.

The man opens an ornate rosewood chest and produces a silver tray on which stands a ruby glass decanter and two crystal goblets. He fills the goblets with wine and offers one to you, saying that the wine will help you forget the unpleasant smell of the workshop.

If you wish to accept his gracious offer, take the goblet and turn to **288**.

If you wish to decline his offer and leave the taxidermy, turn to **279**.

214

The Kalte hunting bow is constructed from many strips of bone, glued and bonded together with layers of sinew. It is an ideal weapon for hunting Baknar or Kalkoth in the icy wastes of Kalte, but as a target bow in the warm climate of the Stornlands it is a very poor choice. When you enter the tournament, you must reduce your COMBAT SKILL by 4 points for the duration of the contest.

To begin the tournament, turn to **340**.

215

No sooner has the pirate dropped dead at your feet than three more of his snarling comrades press forward to avenge his death.

River Pirates: COMBAT SKILL 19   ENDURANCE 28

If you wish to evade combat after 2 rounds, turn to **286**.

If you win the combat, turn to **111**.

216

You concentrate all your powers of Curing, transmitting the warmth created by your Magnakai skill through your hands into the shattered body of the magician. His frail shoulders tremble as he forces himself to whisper once more: 'Brass street . . . Varetta . . . find Gwynian the sage . . . he will help . . . help your quest—'

Turn to **46**.

217

Swiftly you clamber across the broken stones but your hopes of escape are soon dashed when you see the terrifying drop that awaits you on the other side of the castle wall. Reluctantly, you turn to face your pursuer. With only the yawning precipice behind, you have no choice but to stand and face the monster again. Within seconds it appears, snarling and growling horribly as it prepares to tear you limb from limb.

If you wish to leap aside to avoid the Yawshath's attack, turn to **190**.

If you wish to stand your ground and strike it as it attacks, turn to **311**.

As wave after wave of horses thunder across the bridge, you are trampled into the ground.

Your quest and your life end here.

219 – *Illustration XIII (overleaf)*

Suddenly, there is a mighty crash as the hall door is slammed shut. Into the tavern strides a black-browed young lordling, wearing a flamboyant costume of ebony and gold. He makes ceremonious display of removing his velvet cloak and pompously demands food and wine, and it takes three serving girls and the innkeeper to see to his wishes. His manner is so insulting that you are not surprised to see the many scars that disfigure his young face. He must be continually provoking fights and duels.

The lordling chooses to seat himself at a table already occupied by a small, thin, inoffensive old man. Within seconds there is a thunderous outburst of foul language. The lordling grabs the old man by the throat, lifts him one-handedly from his seat and hurls him to the floor. 'You snivelling toad, how dare you sit with me!' he bellows.

Bewildered and frightened, the little man fumbles an apology, but to no avail. The lordling kicks back his chair and towers over the wretch, his hand clasped around the hilt of his sword. The tavern crowd view the scene with relish, like spectators at a Vassagonian arena for the lordling clearly intends to kill the old man.

If you possess a bow, turn to **301**.
If you do not possess a bow, turn to **78**.

XIII. The lordling kicks back his chair and towers over the wretch

220

The weather-worn plaque bolted to the base of the statue says that this is a true likeness of Vynar Jupe who led a band of robbers that preyed on travellers, especially merchants. His many crimes, including murder, did not prevent him from becoming popular, for he was resourceful and daring, and never plundered the inhabitants of this hamlet, where he himself was born. His exploits, and those of a score of his gang, were ended by the executioner's axe after trial at Amory.

There is a slit in the belly of the statue through which Gold Crowns can be dropped. The plaque goes on to say that anyone who pays homage to the statue of Vynar Jupe will be protected by his spirit from robbers and highwaymen.

If you wish to make a donation, place some Gold Crowns into the statue of Vynar Jupe before leaving the hamlet. (Remember to erase however many Gold Crowns you wish to place in the statue from your *Action Chart*.)

Turn to **73**.

221

The soldier removes a spluttering torch from a bracket on the wall and returns to your side. Holding the torch high, he casts his eye over you and your horse and rubs his stubbly chin.

'You come from Varetta or Soren? Long ride either way – you must be tired. In you go, but in future be sure to get a cess – some o' my brother-guards ain't so understanding.'

You thank the guard and ride in through the town gate.

Turn to **129**.

222

The monster dives straight for you from the top of the stairs. You hold your ground and land a well-timed and deadly accurate blow, which opens a gaping wound in the creature's neck, killing it instantly. However, the strength of your blow is not enough to turn its heavy body aside and you cannot avoid being crushed beneath the Yawshath as it hits the flagstones. You lose 12 ENDURANCE points.

If you are still alive, turn to **106**.

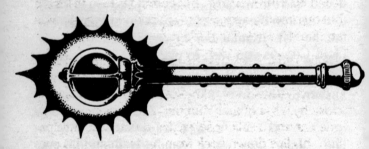

223

Unfortunately, you have lost your bet. The conjurer stated that at least one of the children was lying, and if one was lying the other could not have been telling the truth. The answer is that both children lied.

Erase the Gold Crowns you staked on the conundrum from your *Action Chart*, before approaching the bar and enquiring about a room for the night.

Turn to **253**.

224

'Hell's teeth!' cries the captain. 'Have we run aground?'

As the words leave his lips, a grapnel and rope drop from the sky and bite into the ship's rail. More follow and, through the mist, you can make out the shapes of longboats approaching.

'River pirates!' shouts the helmsman. 'Prepare to repel boarders.'

Further along the deck, one of the captain's men is felled by a thrown knife. His comrades rush to his aid but by now the river pirates are pouring over the side and he is trampled underfoot.

'Battle order!' bellows the captain and immediately his men respond, linking shields and holding their ground. A swarm of grim-faced pirates are boarding close by. One of their number, a lean man with only one ear and a split nose, smiles at you with anticipation, his lips drawn back from his teeth and his eyes wide with excitement. He is obviously relishing the thought of ending your life.

If you have a bow and wish to use it, turn to **170**.
If you wish to prepare for combat by other means, turn to **92**.
If you wish to evade combat, turn to **286**.

225

You rein in your horse beneath the wide stone archway of the south gate. From an arrow slit in the wall echoes a harsh voice: 'Rider, show your pass!'

There is the dull clunk of a bolt being drawn and two swarthy guards dressed in chainmail appear. They eye you suspiciously and repeat the demand to see a pass.

> If you wish to tell them that you do not have a pass, turn to **55**.
>
> If you want to try to ride past them and through the open town gate, turn to **261**.
>
> If you want to attempt to bribe them to let you pass, turn to **9**.

226

You push against the great doors but they will not open – they are locked.

> If you wish to knock on the temple doors, turn to **242**.
>
> If you decide to ignore the temple and enter the observatory, turn to **127**.
>
> If you would rather follow a corridor that runs alongside the temple, turn to **327**.

227

They have covered only a few hundred yards when the last rider turns to check on Cyrilus who is beginning to slip from his saddle. You pull off the highway to try to hide, but you are seen entering the trees and a shout rings out: 'He's there!' The rumble of hooves warns you that the riders are returning.

If you have a bow and wish to open fire as they rush past, turn to **20**.

If you would rather prepare to fight by other means, turn to **203**.

228

The red wine looks and smells delicious. The man must hold you in high esteem, for wine as good as this is rare and expensive.

If you possess the Magnakai Discipline of Curing, turn to **136**.

If you do not have this skill, drink the wine and turn to **84**.

229

The Ogrons are poor archers and in the gathering gloom they fail to drop an arrow within ten feet of you. You paddle across to the far side and as soon as the pontoon grounds on the bank, you slip ashore and creep across the rocks to the sewer outfall.

Turn to **249**.

230

'A toast to our gallant friend,' cries the soldier with the pock-marked face. 'Honour in battle!' shouts the red-haired man to his left. 'And a rich purse for the victor,' retorts the other. They laugh heartily and raise the flagons to their lips. Their smiling faces are completely hidden by the jugs as they drink their fill. A full minute of silence passes before the three jugs are slammed to the table, emptied of ale.

The strong beer soon dissolves any guardedness and

they become very talkative about themselves. You take this opportunity to ask them what they know of the Lorestone of Varetta.

'Legend,' belches the red-head, 'myth or legend.' 'Not so,' interrupts Pock-face. 'It's real enough, but it was lost years ago. The Lorestone is magical – it holds a power that can turn an ordinary man into a king.'

On hearing this, the other soldiers snigger, but Pock-face ignores them and continues. 'The Lorestone was once set into the throne of Lyris, at the Tower of the King in Varetta. Hundreds of years ago, during the War of the Lorestone, it was stolen by a Salonese prince called Kaskor. He set the stone upon a gold sceptre and used it in battle to inspire his followers. He believed that it made him invulnerable, but it was not so. He was killed in a battle on board his royal barge at Rhem, and the Lorestone was lost when it fell from his hand into the depths of the River Storn. However, that is not the end of the story. There are many tales about the sceptre having been found, but on the whole they have turned out to be fake or merely fanciful. The legend says whoever wields the Lorestone is the rightful ruler of all the Stornlands. For this reason above all others, the Lorestone is sought by many evil or unscrupulous men to further their dreams of power. If you wish to know more, you should go to Varetta. There are many learned men who have devoted their lives to the study of the Lorestone – the scholars and sages of Brass Street – they are the people to help you!'

You thank the soldier for his help and take your leave of the company.

If you now wish to order some food, turn to **172**.

If you decide to go to the bar and enquire about a room for the night, turn to **232**.

231

You help the captain to carry his purchases, which fill two large wooden boxes. As you stagger from the apothecary, he tells you he is anxious to return to the boat without delay. His men are good soldiers but poor sailors – he fears that without his watchful eye and stern command they will forget their work and drink themselves into a stupor. His fears are unfounded, for upon your return to the quay the *Kazonara* is fitted out and ready to sail.

'Cast off,' booms the captain, enjoying the novelty of his new riverboat command. 'We'll make Rhem by nightfall.' The captain is as good as his word. As dusk settles over the Storn, you sail into the horseshoe harbour at Rhem.

Turn to **124**.

232– *Illustration XIV*

The innkeeper is a fat, oily individual with small piggish eyes and a crooked smile. A grimy cloth hangs by a cord from his wrist, which he uses to wipe the bar. He seems unconcerned that the filthy rag does little but smear grease further across the counter.

'You are in luck, my friend,' he says, rummaging through the pockets of his striped apron. 'We have one room left – room 17.' He produces a plain iron key and sets it down upon the bar. 'Three Gold Crowns – in advance.'

You pay the innkeeper (remember to erase the Gold Crowns from your *Action Chart*), and slip the key into your pocket. You are contemplating an early night when your rumbling stomach reminds you that you need to eat.

If you wish to take a seat and order some food, turn to **328**.

If you decide to eat a Meal (from your Backpack) in the privacy of your room, you can head towards the stairs by turning to **219**.

233

Instantly, you recognize the old man who stands before you now, calm and smiling. It is the same old man whom you encountered in a hut on the road to Ruanon some years ago; the same man who handed you a scroll that foretold the dangers of the Chasm of Doom.

XIV.   'You're in luck, my friend, we have one room left'

'Welcome, Lone Wolf,' he says. 'Once again the stars have dictated that our paths would cross.'

Turn to **6**.

234

From within the closed helmet of black steel, a voice calls out – 'Die northlander!' The crossbow is hurled aside and the warrior charges out of the Denka Gate, an axe held high in his hand. You cannot avoid him and must fight him to the death. Due to the speed of his attack you cannot use a bow.

Armoured Assassin:

COMBAT SKILL 24   ENDURANCE 26

If you win the combat, turn to **28**.

235

In the dim light of the sewer you can just discern the outlines of the curtain wall and the streets of Tekaro on your map. The cathedral is right in the centre of the city, approximately half a mile from the point where the two rivers meet, and lying due east of the point at which you entered the sewer. You fold the map and set off again towards your objective.

Turn to **269**.

236

The arrow whistles through the gloom and gouges a channel of skin and fur from the creature's skull. It shrieks in pain and paws at the wound. Although it is injured it is far from dead and sharp claws extend from a bloodstained paw. They lash at your head and you duck only just in time to save yourself from decapitation. Hurriedly, you prepare for hand-to-hand combat before the monster strikes again.

Turn to **343**.

237

A crowd have gathered to watch the fight. As you strike the fatal blow, a cheer goes up and they surge forward like vultures, eager to pick the corpse clean. You and your horse are shouldered aside by the greedy mob as they strip the dead man of all his belongings.

Repulsed by their behaviour you quickly turn and ride away from the degrading spectacle.

Turn to **279**.

238

About a hundred yards from the east gate, through which you entered the city, you notice a brass plaque, fixed with polished brass spikes to the top of an arched doorway. The sign reads:

If you wish to dismount and enter the doorway, turn to **25**.

If you do not wish to enter, you can continue to the east gate, where two streets lead away from the gatehouse.

If you wish to take the north street, turn to **79**.

If you wish to take the south street, turn to **147**.

239

As you wait, Cyrilus becomes agitated. You sense that he is scared to be left on his own after his encounter with Roark. 'Are you bound for Varetta?' he asks. 'Perhaps we could share the journey? I am bound for the capital in the morning. I know the road very well and I know its dangers – it would not be wise to travel alone on such a road.'

You pause to consider the prospect of sharing your journey with this old man. On the one hand his company would make the miles seem shorter, but on the other hand, he could prove to be a burden and slow you down. You are about to decline when he says something that convinces you to share the journey.

Turn to **319**.

240

As you walk towards his table, three muscular body-guards suddenly appear and block your path. The merchant looks up from beneath the rim of his floppy velvet hat and says in a thin voice: 'What business do you have with me, stranger?'

If you wish to ask the merchant the way to Brass Street, turn to **47**.

If you say you wish to do some business with him, turn to **189**.

If you decide to apologize for intruding on his privacy and approach the tavern-keeper, turn to **312**.

241

Near the crest of the hill there is a small hut built close to the track. Outside, on the porch, sits an old woman who is peeling fruit with a wooden knife. She smiles a gap-toothed smile and bids you welcome as you bring your horse to a halt.

If you wish to ask her if she has seen any riders pass her home, turn to **110**.

If you decide to ignore her and continue up the track, turn to **3**.

242

A deadly silence descends on the congregation as your knocking echoes around the temple. A key rattles in the lock; slowly the doors open. A hundred pairs of eyes stare at you suspiciously as you enter the sanctum and a priest in golden robes strides towards you along the wide central aisle. His face is red with anger and he demands to know the reason for your intrusion. When you reply that you have come in search of the Lorestone, a loud gasp of horror rises from the crowd.

Suddenly, the doors crash shut. As one, the congregation stand and unsheathe long curved daggers from beneath their dark brown robes. Murder and hatred glint in their eyes as they close in and hack you to pieces.

Your life and your quest end here.

243

The rancid stench of the creature's breath fills your nostrils as you release the bowstring.

Pick a number from the *Random Number Table*. If you have the Magnakai Discipline of Weaponmastery with a bow, add 3 to the number you have picked.

If your total is now *0—3*, turn to **155**.
If it is *4—8*, turn to **292**.
If it is *9—12*, turn to **264**.

244

Your horse is killed instantly in the rain of arrows. As it crashes to the ground you are hurled forwards, somersaulting through the air before landing in a heap on the bloodstained soil. The archers have brought down the first two ranks of horsemen but the attack is still pressing forward over the dead and dying in a reckless stampede towards the gate. You are now lying in the path of this stampede.

If you wish to leap over the parapet of the bridge to avoid the onrushing horses, turn to **38**.

If you wish to curl up into a ball and keep completely still, turn to **218**.

If you wish to run towards the Tekaro Gate, turn to **329**.

245

First, decide how many Gold Crowns you wish to wager and note this down in the margin of your *Action Chart*. You consider the problem and decide that there can only be four possible combinations, and you repeat the conundrum under your breath before making your decision: ' "I'm a boy," said the one with black hair. "I'm a girl," said the one with blond hair.'

If you decide that they both spoke the truth, turn to **50**.

If you decide that the first child spoke the truth and the second child lied, turn to **113**.

If you decide that the first child lied and the second child spoke the truth, turn to **223**.

If you decide that both children lied, turn to **62**.

246

The shambling monster passes within inches of your hiding place but miraculously it does not detect you. Gradually, the sound of its hideous laugh fades into the darkness and you emerge from the alcove and hurry back up the stairs to the surface.

In the chapel you find your glass jar still intact and waste no time filling it with Taunor Water (the healing spa water will restore 6 ENDURANCE points). You may drink the Water now or place the glass jar in your Backpack for future use. (Remember to mark it on your *Action Chart* as a Backpack Item.)

You decide to return to Cyrilus without delay, for the Yawshath is still at large and could attack again at any time.

Turn to **338**.

247

The highway descends into a wide valley that bears the scars of war – derelict cottages, their walls broken and charred, dot the landscape. You cross a stagnant stream by a rickety wooden bridge and climb towards a copse of trees at the brow of a hillock. As you draw closer to the copse you hear a low hypnotic chant coming from somewhere inside the ring of trees.

If you wish to dismount and investigate the sound, turn to **13**.

If you wish to ignore it and continue along the highway to Soren, turn to **102**.

If you have the Magnakai Discipline of Divination, turn to **206**.

248

The guards leap from the wagons and surround you with a ring of spears. Their sergeant steps forward and growls, 'Throw down your weapons, stranger, or we'll feed you to the crows!'

To reinforce this threat, he stabs at your leg with his spear and its sharp tip nicks your thigh.

If you wish to retaliate and attack the sergeant, turn to **201**.

If you have the Magnakai Discipline of Invisibility, turn to **322**.

249

There is a gaping hole in the criss-crossed bars, large enough for you to pass through with ease. The fetid water that is combed by this grille contains all manner of filth, a veritable feast for rats and vermin. However, as you wade deeper into the tunnel, you gradually realize that the sewer is completely free of rats and, in fact, seems to be totally devoid of all life. Circular chutes appear at regular intervals in the tiled ceiling but they are far too small and slippery to climb. Fifteen minutes after entering the sewer, you arrive at a major junction where two new channels flow into the main course.

If you wish to continue ahead, turn to **269**.
If you wish to follow the left channel, turn to **318**.
If you wish to follow the right channel, turn to **339**.
If you have a Map of Tekaro, turn to **235**.

250

You recognize the orange berries of the alether plant. They are much sought after by warriors and soldiers, for they increase both strength and skill during combat.

If you wish to purchase some Alether Berries, turn to **123**.
If you do not or cannot afford to buy any, and decide to remount your horse and leave the village, turn to **100**.

251

The room is a disappointment. For five Gold Crowns you were expecting some degree of luxury, but the small and shabby accommodation you find leaves much to be desired. Steam rising from an open-topped barrel in a corner of the room clouds the air. At first you think it must be some form of heating, until you discover it is full of soapy water and realize that this is, in fact, your hot bath. The meagre luxuries of Varetta do not come cheaply.

You bathe before settling down to a good night's rest but in the middle of the night you are woken by a bright light. A shooting star of sun-like brilliance arcs over the city, shedding a rainbow of colour across your drab room. You watch as the star slowly fades and then settle down to sleep once more. It seems as if you have only just closed your eyes when the loud and loathsome clang of the tavern bell fills your ears.

'All awake, all awake! A new day dawns, my fine brave lads!' As the voice of the tavern-keeper echoes through the inn, you gather your equipment and collect your horse from the stable. The night's rest restores 3 ENDURANCE points. Make the necessary adjustment to your *Action Chart* before setting off on your search for Brass Street.

Turn to **300**.

252

A loud cheer shatters the silence as your arrow strikes home – you have won. The villagers are thrilled to have witnessed such an exciting tournament and crowd around you to offer their praise and congratulations. The little man in the braided jerkin presents you with your prize – a magnificent bow made from the wood of a silver oak tree. This weapon will add 3 points to your total whenever you are using a bow and are instructed to pick a number from the *Random Number Table*. Enter it in the 'Weapons' section of your *Action Chart* as a Silver Oak Bow and make a note of its particular property.

After making a short speech to thank the villagers for their generosity, you shoulder your prize and head back to Cyrilus with the good news.

Turn to **33**.

253

'Looks as like y'made it here jus' in time,' says the cheerful innkeeper, pointing to a rain-streaked window pane. 'It's going' t'be a rough night t'night, no mistakin'.'

You discover that a room for the night costs 2 Gold Crowns, plus 1 Gold Crown for your horse's keep. A Meal of black bread and hard-boiled eggs will cost you another Gold Crown, unless you choose to eat a Meal from your Backpack: you must in any case eat a Meal now or lose 3 ENDURANCE points.

If you wish to pay the innkeeper for a night's lodging, turn to **35**.

If you do not have enough Gold Crowns to pay for a room, turn to **54**.

254

You run across the steering deck and down a stair to the level below, but as soon as your feet touch the bloodstained planks you are attacked from behind by two pirates.

Pirates: COMBAT SKILL 18   ENDURANCE 27

Unless you have the Magnakai Discipline of Hunt-mastery, deduct 2 from your COMBAT SKILL for the first round of this combat.

If you win the combat, turn to **77**.

255

A dull throbbing pain fills your head as the leader's words reach your ears. You sense that you are being attacked by a powerful Mindforce, but your Psi-shield effectively blocks this psychic assault. However, you pretend to be in agony, hoping to make the leader think he has won victory. Everyone in the procession seems to be delighted by your apparent suffering, as if your cries are music to their ears. They press forward, unsheathing hidden daggers as they rush to encircle you.

If you wish to evade their onslaught, turn to **289**.
If you wish to engage in combat with these evil men, turn to **194**.

256

Redbeard takes you to a tavern that looks more like a banqueting hall than a city alehouse. The Inn of the Crossed Swords is the largest and noisiest tavern you have ever seen. A constant flow of soldiers pours in and out of its cathedral-like doors and the stable is large enough to house an entire army's horses. You stable your horse and accompany Redbeard through the massive oak doors.

'Ale for my friend,' he booms and immediately an inn-girl hurries to obey his command. He points to a table across the hall and says with a cheerful voice: 'There he is – come and meet the captain.'

Turn to **211**.

257

The bolt of energy burns through your chest like a red-hot poker. You recoil in pain but can no longer control your movements and are blasted high into the air, impaled upon the end of the crackling bolt. Suddenly, it vanishes, leaving you to plummet one hundred feet on to the hard unyielding stone of the altar.

Your life and your quest end here on the sacrificial altar of the Cener Druids.

258 – *Illustration XV (overleaf)*

A drawbolt is slammed back and the great gate slowly opens. 'At last, Esmond! Did we wake you from your—' Cyrilus chokes in mid-sentence, his eyes wide with shock. Inside the gate sits a warrior on a warhorse, wreathed in armour of black and gold. A crossbow rests across his forearm; it is pointed at you. Without warning, he pulls the trigger and the bolt hisses towards your chest.

If you have the Magnakai Discipline of Divination, turn to **283**.

If you have the Magnakai Discipline of Hunt-mastery, turn to **164**.

If you possess neither of these skills, turn to **97**.

XV. Without warning, the warrior pulls the trigger of his crossbow

259

The door is old and decayed – it has not been opened for a hundred years. If you are to find out what lies beyond it, you will have to clear away the dirt that jams the hinges.

If you have the Magnakai Discipline of Nexus or Psi-surge, turn to **186**.

If you do not have either of these skills, turn to **156**.

260

'We have all the company we need,' sneers a shiny-faced warrior, his cheeks pock-marked by disease. 'State your business or begone, lest our swords grow restless.'

If you choose to introduce yourself, turn to **130**.

If you wish to call their bluff and challenge them to a fight, turn to **159**.

If you decide to ignore them, take a seat elsewhere, and order some food, turn to **172**.

261

You strike the flank of your horse and break through the startled guards in a matter of seconds but as you gallop through the gate, two more appear and block your path. They are armed with long pikes which they slope at your chest. Tightly you rein in your horse to avoid the threatening steel tips.

Pick a number from the *Random Number Table*. If you have the Magnakai Discipline of Animal Control, add 3 to the number you have picked.

If your total is now *0—2*, turn to **99**.

If it is *3—6*, turn to **187**.

If it is 7 or higher, turn to **22**.

262

The green-skinned Kloon stares at you, the trace of a sneer playing on his thick rubbery lips. 'Wait here,' he says off-handedly and waddles out through the door, slamming it shut as he leaves.

If you wish to wait for him to return, turn to **116**.

If you would rather leave the guildhouse and continue on your way, turn to **105**.

If you have the Magnakai Discipline of Divination, turn to **58**.

263

'W . . . w . . . what do you want,' squeals the merchant, cowering behind the edge of the table. His haughty manner has vanished with the lives of his bodyguards and he is shaking with fear.

You push the table aside, grab him by his lapels and hoist him to his feet.

'Relax my friend – I only wish to ask the way to Brass Street,' you say with a laugh.

The merchant looks at you incredulously, the sweat pouring down his ashen face. 'The . . . the . . . the way to Brass Street?' he stammers. 'Of course, of course . . . er, let me show you.'

The terrified little man produces a crumpled piece of parchment and hurriedly scribbles directions to Brass Street. You see that it is located on the far side of the city, close to the west wall. Taking the parchment from his twitching fingers, you bid him goodnight and step over the dead bodies of the guards. There is a sudden crash; the merchant has fainted and fallen flat on his face.

Turn to **17**.

264

The creature stops in mid-stride, as if paralysed by some invisible force. A gurgling croak escapes from its lips and, as it locates your arrow with its trembling paws, it collapses to its knees. Death is but seconds away. It shudders and sways and then keels over on to its back, writhing for one brief moment in the mud and debris of the chapel floor.

Turn to **112**.

265

He screams and falls with the arrow embedded so deeply into his chest that only its feathered flights can be seen. His comrades freeze in their tracks, their eyes wide with fear. As you move forward they scatter and run.

Turn to **77**.

266

The ale is cool and refreshing. (Restore 1 ENDURANCE point.) As you drink, you see that the sleeping barman slouched on his stool is oblivious to your presence. You finish your ale and slam the tankard down, hoping to stir him with the sudden noise, but he does not react. However, you feel you should thank him for his hospitality before leaving the hut.

Turn to **93**.

267

The night passes without sleep; the howling wind of the Varettian plain is your only companion as you ride the long, straight, moonlit highway to Soren. When dawn finally breaks you find yourself on the outskirts of a small and undistinguished hamlet of half-timbered buildings – whose only unusual feature is a bronze statue of a roguish-looking young man that stands in front of the blacksmith's shop.

If you wish to examine the statue, turn to **220**.
If you decide to ignore it and continue on your way to Soren, turn to **73**.

268

The drawstring cuts into your fingers as you take aim at the creature's glowing eyes.

Pick a number from the *Random Number Table*. If you have the Magnakai Discipline of Weaponmastery with a bow, add 3 to the number you have picked.

If your total is now *0—5*, turn to **155**.
If it is *6—8*, turn to **236**.
If it is *9—12*, turn to **75**.

269

A hundred yards along the passage you see a flight of stone steps ascending to a stone trapdoor set flush with the ceiling.

If you wish to investigate the trapdoor, turn to **107**.
If you wish to continue along the sewer, turn to **120**.

Above the church, a whirlpool of darkness is taking form, casting a tomb-like chill on everything beneath. Frost crystalizes on the grass and flowers, and a terrible sound fills the air as the earth begins to shake. Cracks appear in the ground beneath you and suddenly a score of fleshless hands burst through the frozen soil to grab your horse. Shrieking with terror, it rears up and you are thrown into the waiting arms of the waking dead.

Undead Summonation:

COMBAT SKILL 18   ENDURANCE 35

Due to the surprise of the attack, deduct 2 points from your COMBAT SKILL for the first two rounds of combat, unless you have the Magnakai Discipline of Huntmastery. The undead are immune to Psi-surge and Mindblast. Also, unless you possess the Magnakai Discipline of Nexus, you must deduct 2 ENDURANCE points for every round of combat you fight, due to the intense cold.

If you win the combat, turn to **326**.

271

You have barely covered a hundred yards when you hear a frantic cry: 'Horse thief, horse thief! Don't let him get away!'

You tighten your grip and urge the horse along the highway as it dips and bends, following the low hedgerow that borders the tournament field. The cry alerts some men from the archery competition and they soon appear in a line at the edge of the field. As they see you approach, they draw their bows to fire.

XVI. You are thrown into the arms of the waking dead

Pick a number from the *Random Number Table*. If you have the Magnakai Discipline of Animal Control or Huntmastery, add 3 to the number you have picked.

If your total is now 5 or below, turn to **52**.
If your total is now 6 or higher, turn to **81**.

272

The air is sweet with the smell of wet grass. The sun rises above the trees to the east and mist steams from the hills on either side of the highway. By noon you reach a small village, where brightly decorated cottages line a cobblestoned square. A shrine with an enormous onion-shaped dome stands in the middle of the square, and in its shadow sit a group of old women. They are tending to some shrubs with bright orange berries, which grow in the shade.

If you wish to stop and investigate the shrine, turn to **342**.
If you wish to continue on your way to Varetta, turn to **100**.
If you possess the Magnakai Discipline of Curing, turn to **250**.

273

'It's the tax y'gotta pay to enter Amory,' he answers, irritated by your ignorance of local customs. 'This is Lyris and Amory is in Salony,' he explains, emphasizing every word as if you are deaf or dull-witted. 'You . . . will . . . need . . . a . . . Cess . . . to . . . enter . . . Amory.'

If you wish to purchase a Cess, pay him 3 Gold Crowns and turn to **304**.

(contd over)

If you wish to ignore him and continue your
journey, turn to **146**.

If you decide to teach him some manners, turn to
160.

274

You urge your horse forward with expert precision,
taking the jump with deceptive ease. The angry cries
of the guards are now mixed with some cheers from
onlookers who are obviously delighted by your
horsemanship and daring. The town watch in
Quarlen have a reputation for being pompous and
self-important; anyone who can make fools of them
and get away with it is sure to find favour among the
townsfolk. After a while the cheers and curses fade
behind you and you rein in your horse to take stock of
your surroundings.

Turn to **332**.

275

At the end of the street you stop to look in the window
of a tall, half-timbered shop. It contains a fascinating

selection of maps and charts, which detail the various cities and regions of Magnamund. You enter the shop and browse the shelves that line the walls. Three maps in particular attract your interest: a Map of Sommerlund (5 Gold Crowns); a Map of Tekaro (4 Gold Crowns); and a Map of Luyen (3 Gold Crowns).

The maps are Backpack Items. If you wish to buy one or all of them, make the necessary adjustments to your Action Chart before returning to the apothecary.

Turn to **231**.

276

You concentrate your Magnakai power on the warhammer and slowly it rises from the chest of the corpse. You will it to move upwards and as it appears through the gaping hole, you catch hold of it and examine it closely. It is a very fine weapon, wrought of a metal called bronin, which looks exactly like new bronze, but does not tarnish like ordinary alloys of copper and tin. If you wish to keep this Bronin Warhammer, mark it on your Action Chart as a Weapon. When you use it in combat it will add 1 to your COMBAT SKILL.

Satisfied that nothing else of value has been overlooked, you leave the chapel and return to Cyrilus.

Turn to **338**.

277

The man's reactions are lightning fast. He hurls the silver tray at your head and escapes through a curtained arch at the back of the workshop.

If you wish to give chase, turn to **94**.

If you decide to let him go and leave the taxidermy, turn to **279**.

278

You turn your head to see a shambling, blunt-nosed horror emerge from the shadows. It emits a hideous, snickering cry and lashes out with one of its four razor-sharp claws, sending you tumbling backwards across the muddy flagstones. You quickly regain your feet but the surprise attack has opened a gaping wound in your arm. (You lose 3 ENDURANCE points.) The creature's eyes glow with hatred as it shuffles hungrily towards you.

If you have a bow, turn to **198**.

If you do not have a bow, turn to **343**.

279 – *Illustration XVII*

You arrive at a tavern, but one that looks more like a huge banqueting hall than a city alehouse. The Inn of the Crossed Swords is the largest and noisiest tavern you have ever seen. A constant flow of soldiers pour in and out of its cathedral-like doors and the adjoining stable is large enough to house the horses of an entire army.

You stable your horse and enter the tavern just in time to witness a spectacular event. The middle of the hall has been cleared to allow a horse and rider to gallop the full length of the building and bets are being laid on the rider's skill at skewering fruit on the point of his lance. It reminds you of part of the training taught to Kai Lords in preparation for battle but, unlike the Kai horse trials, there is more than just skill and

XVII.   You enter the tavern in time to witness a spectacular event

the honour of the rider at stake here. In a line along the length of the hall kneel ten soldiers from the same regiment as the rider – men accused of cowardice in battle. The fruits the rider must skewer are resting on their heads. If he makes the slightest mistake the men will lose their lives and, more importantly to the mercenaries, all the money the regiment has wagered on the skill of the rider.

If you wish to stake some Gold Crowns on this deadly game, turn to **284**.

If you wish to approach the bar and talk to one of the barmaids, turn to **299**.

If you wish to sit at one of the tables, turn to **316**.

280

You ride along a muddy path running the length of a ridge that overlooks a great stone bridge. High stone walls and a fortified gatehouse rise steeply from the river bank, and the only access to the city is across the bridge.

You stare at the battlements of Tekaro with growing despair, for they bristle with archers and cauldrons of molten lead. The burnt-out hulks of siege towers and the bodies of dead soldiers lie strewn in heaps before the battered city gate. From where you are you can see the cathedral spire silhouetted in the glow of innumerable fires in the centre of Tekaro. If it were not for this accursed war you would be in the crypt in less than an hour.

You see that before you the path dips steeply towards a line of tents erected behind a wall of earth and logs.

They overflow with the wounded from countless assaults across the bridge.

> If you have the Magnakai Discipline of Curing, you may stop and help the wounded men and turn to **42**.
>
> If you do not have this skill, or choose not to use it, you can continue along the path and turn to **70**.

281

'My humble thanks,' says the frail old man as you help him to his feet. 'I am forever in your debt.'

Taking him by the arm, you escort him to his table where he gathers up his scattered belongings. 'My name is Cyrilus. I am a magician,' he says meekly, as if apologizing for some weakness or abnormality. 'I claim no great understanding of the arcane – my talents are modest by any standard. I only dabble in simple tricks, earning my keep with amusements and sleights-of-hand to amuse the courtiers of Varetta.'

Your eyes obviously betray you; the old man is quick to note your sudden interest in the word 'Varetta'.

If you wish to ask him about the Lorestone of Varetta, turn to **83**.

If you do not wish to question him, bid him good-night and turn to **239**.

282

You pull away and unsheathe your weapon in one swift, fluid movement. The dagger grazes your side (lose 1 ENDURANCE point), but you manage to avoid being seriously wounded. Both men sneer maliciously as they close in for the kill. You cannot evade them and must fight them both as one enemy.

Backstabbers: COMBAT SKILL 18   ENDURANCE 25

If you win the combat, turn to **88**.

283

Forewarned by your power your senses are acutely aware of the deadly missile screaming towards your chest. Suddenly, everything seems to be happening in slow motion. You strike at the bolt as it cuts through the air, deflecting it with one blow. Your opponent hurls his crossbow to the ground and from within the closed helmet of black steel a voice cries: 'Die north-lander!'

The warrior charges out of the Denka Gate with an axe held high in his mailed fist. You cannot avoid the attack and must fight him to the death.

Armoured Assassin:
COMBAT SKILL 24   ENDURANCE 26

Due to the speed of the attack you cannot use a bow. If you have the Magnakai Discipline of Animal

Control, you may add 1 point to your COMBAT SKILL
for the duration of the combat.

If you win the fight, turn to **28**.

284

A huge fat-bellied mercenary is standing on a
wooden box near the door, taking bets from the
crowd of gold-hungry soldiers while his assistants are
busy drumming up business in the hall for their
master. One of the grimy-faced boys approaches and
asks you for your stake.

Firstly, decide how many Gold Crowns you wish to
stake on the event and note this sum in the margin of
your *Action Chart* – there is a maximum bet of 10
Gold Crowns. Next, pick a number from the *Random
Number Table* and note this as well. Pick another
number from the *Random Number Table* and add 3
to it.

If the first number from the *Random Number Table* is
higher than the second total, you win the bet.
Multiply your stake money by 2 to determine how
much you have won (the odds are two to one). If the
second number is higher than the first, the rider has
sucessfully skewered all the fruit without killing any of
the men and your stake money is lost.

You may bet up to three times on this game, or quit at
any stage.

If you quit during the event, turn to **336**.
If you bet on all three rounds and have not lost all
   of your Gold Crowns by the end, turn to **347**.
If you lose all your Gold Crowns, turn to **76**.

285

Ahead there is another stone staircase that leads down into the dungeons of Castle Taunor. It is pitch dark and the stench of mould and decay forces you to cover your nose and mouth as you stagger down the steps. The Yawshath follows you, its unnatural gibbering changing in pitch to a maniacal laugh, which makes you shudder with revulsion.

You sense a passage that continues ahead and a small alcove off to your right.

If you wish to continue straight ahead, turn to **192**.
If you wish to hide in the alcove, turn to **69**.

286 – *Illustration XVIII*

You climb a ladder to the steering deck, drawing your legs up just in time to avoid a razor-sharp cutlass, which slices through the wooden rungs like a hot knife through lard. At the end of the gangway, one of the boat's crewmen is in combat with a pirate, but he is no match for the wiry pirate who dispatches him quickly with a knife. The pirate then catches sight of you and snatches a fresh blade from the bandolier of daggers strapped across his chest. The gangway offers no cover and the pirate's hand is drawn back ready to throw.

If you have the Magnakai Discipline of Hunt-mastery, turn to **314**.
If you do not possess this skill, turn to **142**.

287

You leave your horse tied to a post beside the hut and approach the door. Cyrilus is announcing his arrival

XVIII.   The pirate's hand is drawn back ready to throw

by rapping on the Denka Gate with his staff and shouting to his brother to open up. You chuckle at his growing impatience as he hammers at the gate; if his brother is anything like Cyrilus, he is probably fast asleep.

Inside the hut you are greeted by the mouth-watering smell of freshly baked bread. Pyramids of loaves are stacked high in hampers and trays of pies, flans, cakes and biscuits cover the counter. There is nobody here but an open door reveals another room at the back of the hut.

If you wish to call for service, turn to **43**.
If you wish to help yourself to some bread and cakes, turn to **157**.

288

The wine smells delicious – the taxidermist must hold you in very high esteem for wine as good as this is expensive and rare.

If you possess the Magnakai Discipline of Curing, turn to **61**.
If you do not possess this skill, drink the wine and turn to **84**.

289

Galloping along the narrow thoroughfare through broken streets and dark alleyways, you soon out-distance any immediate threat to your safety. You halt at a small square to allow your horse to drink from a water-trough that stands beside a narrow stone arch. As she drinks her fill, you observe the to-ing and fro-ing of the townsfolk and hear the drunken songs and revelry from the wineshops bordering the square. A knot of brawling rivermen tumble out of one doorway and set about each other with knives and bottles, egged on by their rowdy comrades who wager fistfuls of crowns on the outcome. The fight soon gets out of hand; as it spreads, you decide it is better to leave before you are drawn into it.

Turn to **332**.

You ride into Eula at the captain's side, his banner emblazoned with a flaming battle-axe fluttering overhead. The town has been turned into a huge army encampment; its people have long since fled to the north, abandoning their homes and livestock to the gold-hungry soldiers. Men from a dozen nations rub shoulders with warriors of less-than-human origins, united by common greed. The captain turns to the south where the highway is clogged with foot soldiers. As you catch your first glimpse of Tekaro, burning beneath a pall of black smoke, your heart sinks. This is where the Lorestone lies, in a city under siege from an army of ten thousand fighting men.

As you approach a tangle of siegeworks at the bank of the River Quarl, the captain points to an encampment in a field to your left where a blue flag with a gold eagle flutters in the soot-laden air.

'Prince Ewevin's standard,' he says. 'The time has come to meet our paymaster.'

292

If you wish to stay with the captain's company, turn to **204**.

If you decide the time has come for you to leave the mercenaries, turn to **280**.

291

At first they pretend not to have noticed you, but eventually a stubbly-faced soldier deigns to answer. 'Let the dice decide,' he says, his face red and glowing in the light of the lantern. He raises his hand, spits on his palm and throws the bone dice against the wall.

Pick a number from the *Random Number Table*.

If the number you have picked is *0—4*, turn to **177**.

If the number is *5—9*, turn to **309**.

292

Your feathered shaft cuts the air and sinks deep into the creature's shoulder. It shrieks in pain and snaps the arrow in two with one swipe of its gigantic paw. Although you have injured the beast, it is far from dead. Sharp claws stained with blood lash back at your head and you duck only just in time to save yourself from decapitation. Hurriedly, you prepare for combat.

Turn to **343**.

293

As the door creaks open, a sun-like radiance pours from the tomb and floods the crypt with golden light, its searing intensity paralysing the Dakomyd. You grasp the Lorestone and your senses reel with new-found wisdom and strength. Instinctively, you raise your weapon and strike the monster at the base of its hideous skull. It shrieks and dies instantly.

Turn to **350**.

294

Suddenly, you notice the skeletal badges that adorn the cloaks of these men and a chilling memory floods into your mind. They are dressed identically to the evil priests who accompanied the renegade warlord, Barraka, at the buried temple of Maaken – they are the Acolytes of Vashna.

After the defeat of Barraka, they fled south to escape the Sommlending army. It was a common belief in the Lastlands that the brotherhood had been destroyed and their power extinguished forever but this encounter proves otherwise. You sense that you are in deadly danger. Should they discover your true identity, they will do their utmost to destroy you.

Their leader repeats his demand, his voice sharp with impatience.

> If you wish to answer his question with the reply 'believer', turn to **67**.
> If you choose to say 'unbeliever', turn to **108**.

295

You spring aside just in time to avoid the crackling charge but no sooner has it shot past you than another is sent on its way.

> If you possess the Sommerswerd, turn to **321**.
> If you do not possess this Special Item and wish to attack the leader, turn to **257**.
> If you would rather turn and flee, turn to **182**.

296

The arrow is on target but it does not penetrate the thick metal plates of armour that protect the warrior's back. You watch with dismay as it glances away and disappears over the parapet of the bridge.

Without further delay, you shoulder your bow and mount your horse in order to pursue the kidnappers before they vanish from sight.

> Turn to **39**.

297

The tide of battle has turned in your favour. The pirates came in search of easy plunder but your furious resistance has broken their nerve. They flee from the decks, scrambling into the longboats to escape. The captain follows them, hewing at them with his sword. He cuts his way to the ship's rail and grabs the pirate leader by the neck. He rams the man's head against the main mast, once, twice, three times, with a rage that splits the timber and the pirate's leather-clad skull.

'Ha!' he cries gleefully, 'I've always said the Deldenians have no head for a fight!'

The battle ends as swiftly as it began, with the surviving pirates melting away like phantoms into the fog. There are few casualties amongst the mercenaries but the boat's crew have been decimated. The pirate berserkers trapped them below decks and slaughtered them – only one escaped their murderous blades.

The captain takes command, marshalling repairs and overseeing the burial of the dead. As the bodies sink beneath the dark waters, the *Kazonara* emerges from the mist to the welcoming sight of Luyen.

Turn to **19**.

298

The Jakan is a longbow used by the coastal fishermen of Vassagonia. It is ideally suited to the hunting of barbidahn and squid that live in the shallows and reefs of Barrakeesh, but it is a very poor target bow. In addition to this handicap, the particular bow that you have chosen has a hairline fracture running along its entire length and could well break at any moment.

When you enter the tournament, you must reduce your COMBAT SKILL by 2 points. Also, if at any time you should pick a *0* from the *Random Number Table* when using the bow, the Jakan will break. If this happens during the tournament at any stage, turn immediately to **335**. Make a note of this adventive number in the margin of your *Action Chart* for future reference.

To begin the tournament, turn to **340**.

299

Patiently you wait for one of the overworked tavern girls to notice you but before you can raise your hand and attract her attention, you are suddenly aware of the sharp point of a dagger being pressed against your spine.

'Your purse or your life,' whispers the swarthy-faced mercenary who has appeared at your side. 'Make your mind up quickly or my friend may be a little careless with his knife.'

If you wish to hand over all your Gold Crowns without offering any resistance to the robbers, turn to **161**.

- If you have no Gold Crowns, or if you decide to refuse these men their demand and fight them, turn to **282**.
- If you have the Magnakai Discipline of Hunt-mastery, turn to **114**.

300

As you ride west along a wide avenue of weathered red stone, you take in the early morning sights of this magnificent city. Window shutters slam open as the Varettians awake to a new day and smells of breakfast and freshly ground jala waft from shop doorways.

At the centre of the city you cross a square paved with crystal slabs and pass beneath an archway of polished green stone. Stately halls and public buildings give way to dust-worn shops and a park full of glistening flowers with huge leaves of red, gold and pink. Beyond the park, a street paved with white gravel leads to a fortified tower, the tallest in the city. It is the Tower of the King and marks the entrance to Brass Street.

Turning into Brass Street, the sound of bubbling water and quiet chanting drifts towards you on the still air. Old men in brown robes, their heads covered by hoods, glide silently across the white gravelled path. You ride under an archway and enter the enclosed courtyard of a grand building, a hall of learning. Suddenly, a tingle runs the length of your spine as you sense you are close to your goal.

At the door to the hall there is a sign that indicates the location of three chambers: the observatory, the library and the temple.

If you wish to investigate the observatory, turn to **127**.

If you wish to investigate the library, turn to **21**.

If you wish to investigate the temple, turn to **320**.

301

With the speed and grace of movement that marks you as a Kai Master, you load, take aim and fire. Your arrow pierces the lordling's forearm as his sword descends, causing the blow to splinter stone, not skull. He utters a shrill cry and spins backwards, cradling his wounded arm as he falls.

'Curse you, scum!' he shrieks, 'I am Roark, highborn of Amory. I shall have your life for this – mark my words!'

Trembling with pain and fury, he staggers to his feet and demands his sword and cloak from the innkeeper before stumbling into the night with a welter of threats and curses.

Turn to **281**.

302

The books are catalogued under headings that cover all manner of subjects. You search for those relating to the Lorestone of Varetta, or any that detail the history of the Kai or Sun Eagle's quest. You discover to your surprise that they have all been removed. Judging by the lack of dust on the empty shelves, they were taken away less than a day ago. After double-checking that you have not overlooked anything, you decide that there is little here to help you on your quest and leave the library.

If you now wish to investigate the temple, turn to **320**.

If you decide to enter the observatory, turn to **127**.

303

Your arrow strikes home with deadly accuracy, penetrating the rider's armour at the base of his skull. You see him throw both arms into the air, topple from the saddle and land with a crash of buckled metal in the middle of the bridge. There is no doubt in your mind that your enemy is dead; if the arrow did not kill him then such a fall in heavy armour most surely did.

If you wish to search the body, turn to **139**.

If you wish to mount your horse and pursue the kidnappers, turn to **39**.

304

The youth snatches your gold, flicks the square of blue card at you and slams shut the outhouse door. It is stamped with today's date and will allow you access to the town of Amory on this day only. You pocket the Cess (mark it as a Special Item on your *Action Chart*), and leave.

Turn to **146**.

305

Once through the arch, you run headlong across a rock-strewn courtyard towards a breach in the castle wall. Here you notice a stone staircase leading down to an iron gate. A quick glance over your shoulder tells you that the Yawshath is still in hot pursuit and is closing the gap. It is in a frenzy of hatred and anger.

If you wish to climb through the breach in the castle wall, turn to **217**.

If you wish to run down the stairs to the iron gate, turn to **169**.

If you have the Magnakai Discipline of Divination, turn to **122**.

306

Desperately, you fight against the current and claw your way towards the bank. Breathless, freezing and soaking wet, you stagger from the water and collapse on the rocks. Unless you have the Magnakai Discipline of Nexus, you lose 1 ENDURANCE point due to extreme cold.

As your senses return, you find that you have emerged from the river close to where the Quarl joins the River Storn. You see a small cave in the base of the city wall less than twenty feet from where you lie, a rusty criss-cross of iron covering its mouth. Judging by the foul smell of the water pouring from its depths, you suspect it to be a sewer outfall. Suddenly, a flicker of hope returns as you realize that this outfall could lead right into the heart of Tekaro.

Turn to **249**.

307

A wagon draws up beside an empty fountain. Its tailgate flaps down to reveal a cargo of freshly baked bread and a rush of hungry soldiers flood round like bees to honey, desperate to buy some of the mouth-watering fare. You have not eaten today and the delicious smell wakens your sleeping appetite. The loaves are 2 Gold Crowns each, and each loaf counts as one Meal. You may purchase as many loaves as you wish. Unless you eat a Meal now you must lose 3 ENDURANCE points. Make the necessary adjustments to your *Action Chart*.

Turn to **279**.

308

Your Magnakai skill tells you the meaning of a symbol carved into the stone above the south gatehouse: it is a winged spur, the emblem of the army of Lyris. This gate must be the entrance to a guardhouse, for the highway that leads to the north gate shows signs of more frequent use where its deeply rutted surface has borne the brunt of merchant traffic to and from Casiorn. The tracks that mark the road here are only those of iron-shod horses. As the border guards of Lyris have a poor reputation for hospitality, it would be wise to avoid them if possible.

If you wish to approach the north gate, turn to **137**.

If you decide to approach the south gate, turn to **225**.

309

'Whoa! T'is not your lucky night, stranger. The dice command me to hold my tongue.'

He and his swarthy companions turn their backs on you and laugh as they continue their game. You shrug your shoulders and press on along the crowded street.

Turn to **307**.

310

The crypt floor is crawling with the severed remains of the monster, which still writhe blindly forward with maniacal intent. Spider-like, a severed hand climbs your leg and embeds its talons in your flesh. (You lose 2 ENDURANCE points.) As you fight to free yourself from its vice-like grip, the torn pieces of the Dakomyd's body gather themselves together for another attack.

If you wish to leap forward and strike the creature before it has completely formed, turn to **323**.

If you wish to unlock the tomb and retrieve the Lorestone, turn to **293**.

311

Blind with hate and rage, the Yawshath dives straight at you. Your blow is well timed and deadly accurate – it opens a deep gash in the creature's torso, killing it instantly. However the strength of your blow is not enough to turn aside the creature's body; it smashes into your chest, carrying you over the edge of the precipice to your doom.

Your quest and your life end here.

312

You find the tavern-keeper breaking up a fight between two drunken soldiers. His solution to their argument is short and sweet: grabbing the two men by their necks, he slams their heads together with such force that the crack echoes above the deafening clamour of the hall.

'Brass Street?' he replies, his face lined in thought, 'yes, I know it well. Here, I'll show you.' The big man produces a greasy piece of paper from his pocket on which he scrawls the directions to Brass Street. You see that it is located on the far side of the city, close to the west wall. You accept the paper and the tavern-keeper accepts your thanks before returning to the crowd to sort out another scuffle in his own inimitable way.

Turn to **17**.

313

You gasp with shock as the bolt sinks deeply into your shoulder (lose 8 ENDURANCE points), and fight to stay in the saddle as the force of impact throws you to one side.

If you are still alive after this grievous wounding, turn to **234**.

314

You crouch in readiness to avoid the dagger whistling towards your chest. Your eye follows the glinting blade, anticipating its path with perfect accuracy. The pirate gasps with amazement as you run straight towards the dagger, twisting aside at precisely the right second for the blade to pass beneath your raised arm. Unnerved by the shock, he is unprepared for your attack and before he can recover himself, he is tumbling backwards over the side of the boat into the cold, deep waters of the Storn.

Turn to **254**.

315

A blistering pain erupts in your head as the leader's curse reaches your ears. You are being attacked by a powerful Mindforce, which robs you of 4 ENDURANCE points.

The procession are obviously delighted by your suffering – your cries seem to be music to their ears. They press forward, unsheathing hidden daggers from their robes as they try to encircle you. Mustering your reserves of strength, you turn your horse round and gallop away, desperate to put distance between yourself and the source of your agony.

Turn to **332**.

316

You are about to draw a chair out from under the table and sit down when you suddenly freeze: the sharp point of a dagger is being pressed against your spine.

'Your purse or your life,' whispers the swarthy-faced mercenary who has appeared at your side. 'Make your mind up quickly or my friend may become rather careless with his knife.'

If you wish to hand over all your Gold Crowns without offering any resistance, turn to **161**.

If you have the Magnakai Discipline of Hunt-
mastery, turn to **114**.

If you have no Gold Crowns, or if you decide to
refuse these men their demand and fight them,
turn to **282**.

317

You race out of the hut to see your travelling
companion struggling with six armoured horsemen.
They have him surrounded and his attempts at
resistance are futile. A blow from a mace knocks him
unconscious and he limply falls across the neck of his
horse. A moment later, all but one of the riders are
galloping across the bridge with their captive in tow.
The remaining horseman, a warrior swathed from
head to toe in black and gold armour, raises a crossbow and takes aim as you run towards your horse.

Pick a number from the *Random Number Table*. If
you have the Magnakai Discipline of Divination or
Huntmastery, subtract 5 from the number you have
picked.

If your total is now 6 or less, turn to **85**.
If your total is now 7 or higher, turn to **153**.

318

The channel gradually begins to curve to the east and you notice that it is becoming lighter. You see that a greenish-glow emanates from a vault in the distance, where a curtain of thin, web-like strands hang from the ceiling. If you are to continue in this direction you will have to pass through the curtain.

If you wish to pass through the curtain of strands, turn to **349**.

If you wish to draw them aside with your weapon before passing through, turn to **4**.

If you have the Magnakai Discipline of Animal Control, turn to **32**.

319

'You seek the Lorestone, do you not?' he says, in a hushed tone. 'I cannot tell you where it is, but I know a man who can. Let me ride with you to Varetta and in return I shall take you to this man.'

Your basic Kai instincts tell you that this man speaks the truth. You nod your agreement and arrange to meet in the tavern courtyard at dawn.

Turn to **5**.

320

As you approach the great doors of the temple, you hear the strident voice of a man preaching to a congregation. His words are echoed at intervals by a chorus of voices.

If you wish to enter the temple, turn to **226**.

If you wish to enter the observatory, turn to **127**.

If you have the Magnakai Discipline of Pathsmanship or Divination, turn to **195**.

321

You shudder as the Sommerswerd drinks raw power from the leader's golden rod. His fury turns to fear as you whirl it around your head and hurl the bolt of energy back at his face. There is a tremendous roar as the man disintegrates, consumed in a ball of white flame. However, as you move forwards, you see that each hooded man has a golden rod. They raise them in unison, pooling their collective power to try to destroy your sword.

If you wish to continue your attack, turn to **257**.

If you wish to turn and flee, turn to **182**.

322

'My humble apologies, sergeant,' you say, hoping to avoid confrontation and the possibility of a fight. 'After so many years away from home, I am impatient to see my family.'

The sergeant lowers his spear but continues to eye you suspiciously. Using your Magnakai Discipline of Invisibility, you have imitated the thin nasal sound of the Quarlen dialect to perfection, but the sergeant is still wary. However, he gradually relaxes his guard and the sneer is replaced by a smile on his battle-scarred face.

'We have a special toll for the likes of you who forget

their native manners – 10 Gold Crowns,' he says, a gloved hand held out in expectation.

If you wish to pay the sergeant 10 Gold Crowns, turn to **332**.

If you choose not to pay and decide to evade the sergeant while his guard is down by jumping the wagons, turn to **72**.

323

The Dakomyd shudders and reels back as your weapon makes impact, sinking deep into flesh that clings like jelly and reeks of a charnel smell that closes your throat. A drop of its watery blood splashes on your arm, eating through your tunic and searing your flesh. Your weapon disintegrates, corroded by the blood. Before you can pull away, a razor-sharp talon snares your cloak and draws you to your doom.

Your life and your quest end here in the crypt of Tekaro Cathedral.

324 – Illustration XIX

Tearing aside the curtain, you rush into a high-vaulted chamber that reeks of preservatives and dead bodies. From hooks in the ceiling hang the carcasses of exotic animals, and on the many work tables lie dissected heads, destined for trophy plaques. You cast your eyes around the workshop but the man has vanished.

If you have the Magnakai Discipline of Divination or Huntmastery, turn to **208**.

If you do not possess either of these skills, turn to **37**.

XIX.   The chamber reeks with the pungent smell of preservatives
and dead bodies

325

You do not have to look very far for the horse's owner – at this very moment he is striding towards you. Suddenly, he recognizes you and salutes you with a friendly wave.

If you won the archery contest, turn to **45**.
If you did not win the archery contest, turn to **132**.

326

As you destroy the last of the fleshless skeletons, you see that the struggle has spread beyond the walls of the churchyard. From the depths of an open crypt, a shambling mass of zombies are hurling themselves at the riders, tearing the terrified warriors from their saddles. Roark's summonation has gone horribly out of control; no living creature is safe from the terror he has unleashed.

The lordling turns and gallops away in blind panic, leaving his followers to their grisly deaths. As he disappears, the swirling funnel of darkness slowly fades and the undead stagger and fall, crumbling into dust, which is carried away on the evening breeze.

You rush to the aid of the old magician, who lies, mortally wounded, pinned beneath the body of his dead horse. As you cradle his head in your hands, his eyes flicker and open and he forces a whisper from his blood-flecked lips:

'Brass . . . Street . . .'

If you have the Magnakai Discipline of Curing, turn to **216**.
If you do not possess this skill, turn to **46**.

327

You soon come to a junction where two doors face each other across the corridor. The sound of the preacher is drifting through the keyhole of the door to your right, which suggests that access to the temple lies that way. The left door has no keyhole, but you sense that it is not locked.

If you wish to listen at the right door, turn to **195**.
If you wish to enter the left door, turn to **127**.

328

Taking a seat that offers a good view of the hall, you catch the eye of a serving girl and order a plate of roast beef. She returns with a platter stacked high with steaming meat and sets it down before you.

'2 Gold Crowns, if you please, sir,' she says, presenting an open hand that is bloodied by the food. You pay the girl (remember to deduct the Gold Crowns from your *Action Chart*), and settle down to your feast.

Turn to **219**.

329

A hail of arrows engulfs you and an agonizing explosion of pain fills your head, chest and legs. You are mortally wounded and although you fight for your life, the struggle is soon over as you are trampled into the Tekaro Bridge by the captain's men.

Your quest and your life end here.

330

As you reach the junction with the highway, you see the riders emerging in single file behind a derelict cottage. They draw themselves into a circle in the middle of the village and, although they are out of earshot, you can tell by their movements and frantic gestures that they are having a heated argument. Suddenly, the circle breaks and they ride towards you with Cyrilus, still unconscious, in tow behind the last rider. You urge your horse off along the track and take cover among the dense trees.

If you have a bow and want to ambush them as they ride past your hiding place, turn to **20**.

If you wish to attack the last rider and try to recapture Cyrilus, turn to **203**.

If you decide to let them pass and then follow them, turn to **227**.

331

You ride all night without sleep, with only the moon to light your way, and the howling wind as your companion. As the first light of dawn creeps over the horizon you see a small village less than a mile ahead. A dog barks gruffly at you as you ride into the refuse-strewn streets and you are forced to drive it away with the toe of your boot as it snaps persistently at your horse's hind legs.

On the far side of the village, where the highway enters a line of scattered hills, a fortified manor house stands guard. A large sign, faded by wind and rain, proclaims a curious message:

AMORY CESS — 3 GOLD CROWNS

If you wish to stop and enquire at the manor house
about the meaning of the sign, turn to **27**.

If you decide to ignore the sign and continue on
your way to Amory, turn to **146**.

332

You enter a wide street where black iron lanterns
swing above the doors of shops and houses, their oily
black smoke staining the walls and adding a pall of
gloom to the darkening sky. The street descends
towards the River Quarl, where flatboats lie moored
at the rich merchant wharfs. Quarlen stands at the
most northerly point on the river that can be
navigated by boat and barge and it is here that the
river meets the caravan routes to Casiorn and the
Lastlands, so ensuring the future of the town.

At the approach to a wide stone bridge, you see an
impressive-looking hostelry, with stables and out-
houses. A painted shield hangs above the courtyard
gate proudly displaying its name:

THE BARREL BRIDGE TAVERN

The moment you enter the courtyard, a stableboy
appears from nowhere and bids you welcome. He

takes charge of your horse and shows you the door to the tavern hall. It is crowded, despite the early hour, and a roaring fire blazes in its great stone hearth. The smell of roasting beef makes your mouth water, reminding you that you have not eaten today.

If you wish to take a seat and order some food, turn to **172**.

If you wish to approach the bar and ask about a room for the night, turn to **232**.

If you do not have any Gold Crowns, turn to **91**.

If you possess the Magnakai Discipline of Pathsmanship or Divination, turn to **346**.

333

You are about to place a Gold Crown in the woman's hand when a man appears as if from nowhere. He slaps her grubby palm with a studded gauntlet and bellows: 'Begone, y'thievin' hag!'

The woman's eyes flash angrily as she nurses her bruised hand.

If you take exception to this and wish to attack the man, turn to **71**.

If you wish to demand an explanation for his actions, turn to **154**.

If you decide to ride away and avoid a confrontation, turn to **279**.

334

A huge lumbering monster stalks towards you. It is over ten feet high with thick, twisted, hairy limbs and eight-fingered hands tipped by razor-sharp talons. Baleful, monstrous eyes protrude from yellow slits in its glistening head and a long reptilian tail whips behind it. Its hideous and peculiar gibbering fills the moonlit crypt as it draws nearer and nearer.

If you wish to prepare for combat, turn to **344**.
If you have a bow and wish to use it, turn to **209**.

335

A loud crack echoes around the tournament field as the Jakan splits in two. The crowd howl with laughter, and even the stern-faced Altan has to try hard not to chuckle at your misfortune. The little man in the braided jacket informs you that you have lost the tournament by default and announces that Altan is the winner. As the woodsman disappears from sight amongst the teeming crowds of cheering villagers, you take the opportunity to slip away unnoticed and head back towards Cyrilus and the horses.

Turn to **33**.

336

Pushing your way through the crowds of cheering soldiers, you manage to reach a quieter corner of the tavern hall at one end of the immense bar.

If you wish to talk to one of the barmaids, turn to **299**.
If you wish to sit at one of the tables, turn to **316**.

337

Suddenly, a dozen grim-faced robbers spring up from behind the churchyard wall. The wounded man straightens himself and unsheathes a rusty scimitar, an evil cackle issuing from his black-toothed mouth.

The robbers vault the stone wall and run at you, brandishing their tarnished weapons above their heads.

Grave Robbers: COMBAT SKILL 17   ENDURANCE 32

Due to their numbers, you may only evade in the first round of combat.

> If you wish to evade by galloping away towards the west, turn to **191**.
>
> If you stay and win the fight, turn to **40**.

338

A shock awaits you at the top of the hill track. Staring down into the valley below, you see your travelling companion embroiled in a struggle with six armoured horsemen. They have him surrounded and his attempts at resistance are shortlived. You see him struck on the back of the head and fall across the neck of his horse. A moment later the riders are galloping away with their unconscious captive, heading off along the highway to the west.

By the time you reach the base of the track the riders are dots on the horizon. You sprint towards your horse, intent on giving chase before they disappear from view completely and, as you take hold of the reins, you notice Cyrilus' oaken staff lying on the ground. You retrieve the staff before setting off in pursuit of your companion.

Turn to **39**.

339

Slowly, the level of the sewer water begins to drop as you climb a ramp that leads to a circular vault. You stop at the edge of the vault, sensing a pit in the darkness ahead.

If you possess a Kalte Firesphere, a Torch, or a Tinderbox, turn to **80**.

If you do not have any of these Items, turn to **90**.

340

A small, flat-faced man dressed in a silver-braided jerkin, enters the tent and calls for everyone's attention. Quickly, he explains the rules that govern the tournament and then ushers you on to the range. At the far end of the field are a line of targets, each with ten coloured rings marked 0—9. Each archer is given 3 arrows with which he must get a minimum score of 8 in order to qualify for the next round of the tournament.

Pick three numbers from the *Random Number Table* and add them together. If you have the Magnakai Discipline of Weaponmastery with a bow, add 3 to your total.

If your total score is now 7 or less, turn to **103**.

If your total score is now *8* or higher, turn to **26**.

341

With your horse stabled safely in the hold of the *Kazonara*, all that remains for you to do is find your cabin. This proves to be a tiny room at the bow, but at least it has a comfortable bunk and you fall asleep as soon as your head touches the feather pillow.

You wake an hour after dawn and peer out of the circular porthole at the shadowy riverbank. Drizzle obscures all detail and the sky is tinged with grey. As day approaches, the river mist grows thicker and whiter and you go up on deck. The captain stands alone at the rail, the shoulders of his leather cloak soaked by the cold drizzle. He nods a welcome and points to the Cener mountains now hidden in the mist.

'This foul weather robs us of landmarks, but by my reckoning we should be in Luyen by noon.' You stare through the grey, damp air and pull your cloak closely around your shoulders.

If you have completed the Lore-circle of Solaris (that is, you possess the Magnakai Disciplines of Invisibility, Huntmastery and Pathsmanship), turn to **131**.

If you have not completed this Lore-circle, turn to **44**.

342

The women smile as you dismount and approach the shrine.

'Welcome brave sir, welcome to the Shrine of the Warrior. You come in search of our sacred crop, do you not?' says a rosy-cheeked matron, as she dusts the leafy shrubs with a square of silk.

'The fruit of our Alether plant will give you strength in battle,' says another, and offers you a handful of the small orange berries.

If you wish to purchase some Alether berries, turn to **123**.

If you wish to decline her offer, remount your horse and leave the village, turn to **100**.

343

You prepare to defend yourself, for there is no time to evade the creature's attack.

Yawshath: COMBAT SKILL 22   ENDURANCE 38

If you survive 3 rounds of combat and wish to evade the creature by escaping through the archway by which you entered, turn to **305**.

If you win the combat, turn to **112**.

344

The hideous creature gurgles with anger and springs forward to attack.

Dakomyd: COMBAT SKILL 25   ENDURANCE 50

It is immune to Psi-surge and Mindblast.

If you reduce its ENDURANCE to 25 or less, do not continue combat but instead turn to **310**.

345

The man delights in showing you his work, which is excellent. Many of his exhibits were caught on hunting expeditions, either by himself or by clients who wished to preserve their kills as trophies – several trophies have been expertly restored to cover the evidence of wounds or severed limbs. He offers to show you his workshop where these miracles of taxidermy are carried out.

If you wish to see the taxidermist's workshop, turn to **213**.

If you wish to decline his generous offer and leave the shop, turn to **149**.

346

Seated near to the fireplace are three surly-faced drinkers, their tunics stained with the grime of travel. Each wear a red badge upon their breast, embroidered with the crossed swords of Varetta. You sense that they are soldiers-of-fortune, probably in the pay of a captain who comes from the same city.

If you wish to join the men and perhaps find out more about Varetta, turn to **125**.

If you decide not to approach them and wish to go to the bar and ask about a room for the night, turn to **232**.

If you would rather take a seat and order some food, turn to **172**.

347

Your betting has attracted some unwanted attention. Two shifty-eyed mercenaries have been watching you with more than casual interest since your arrival at the Inn of the Crossed Swords and, as the event ends and the crowds disperse, you suddenly feel the sharp point of a dagger piercing the back of your tunic.

'Your purse or your life,' whispers one of the men, his foul breath filling your nostrils. 'Make your choice.'

If you wish to hand over all your Gold Crowns without offering any resistance, turn to **161**.

If you decide to refuse the men their demand and wish to fight to keep your gold, turn to **282**.

If you have the Magnakai Discipline of Hunt-mastery, turn to **114**.

348

You manouevre the noose until it catches on the spur at the back of the hammer's head and lift it gently from the corpse's chest. Unfortunately, the rope is not secure and the warhammer slips from the noose as you pull it upwards. With a dull splash, the weapon lands in one of the black puddles and sinks from sight. Disappointed by such a stroke of bad luck, you retrieve your Rope and coil it back into your Backpack before returning to Cyrilus.

Turn to **338**.

349

You part the strands and step into the small vault beyond, but you have barely set one foot down before you sense that something is wrong. The floor feels soft and spongy and the strands are now coiling themselves around your shoulders. You have stepped into the spawning chamber of a Dakomyd.

As the acid secreted by the larvae eats through your clothes and sears your flesh, you hear the distant mocking laughter of the Dakomyd mother.

Your life and your quest end here.

350– *Illustration XX (overleaf)*

Before your eyes the Dakomyd's skin ripples as if a wave were washing beneath its skin. Suddenly a criss-cross of wrinkles appears and layers of transparent bone peel and fall from its shell-like skull. Its body becomes hunched, shrinking and folding by the second, until all that is left is a film of dust on the floor of the crypt. Time has at last caught up with this ancient terror.

As the golden light begins to fade you stare at the object of your quest – the Lorestone of Varetta. But all that you hold in your hand is a hollow sphere of glass, transparent and unremarkable to look at.

Your quest has succeeded, for the power of the Lore-stone has been transfused into your body and mind. Its strength and wisdom is now a part of you and the transfusion signals the beginning of a new and deadly challenge on your quest for the Magnakai.

But be warned! The quest will draw you into a sinister realm where a malicious and terrible evil has grown in power since Sun Eagle first completed the Magnakai quest. If you possess the courage of a true Kai Master, the challenge and the quest await you in Book 7 of the Lone Wolf series entitled:

CASTLE DEATH

XX.   Time has at last caught up with this ancient terror

Joe Dever

LONE WOLF ADVENTURES

If you're a keen adventure gamebook player, then you should try some of our other bestselling Lone Wolf gamebooks. They are available in bookshops or they can be ordered directly from us. Just complete the form below and enclose the right amount of money and the books will be sent to you at home.

Joe Dever and Gary Chalk

If you would like to order books, please send this form, and the money due to:

ARROW BOOKS, BOOKSERVICE BY POST, PO BOX 29, DOUGLAS, ISLE OF MAN, BRITISH ISLES. Please enclose a cheque or postal order made out to Arrow Books Ltd for the amount due including 30p per book for postage and packing both for orders within the UK and for overseas orders.

NAME ....

ADDRESS ....

....

Please print clearly.

From Joe Dever, author of the award-winning Lone Wolf adventures, comes a major new development in gamebook design.

COMBAT HEROES – DUAL ADVENTURES

Each individual book contains two separate adventures. One you play by yourself, the other you play with a copy of the twin book and a friend!

If you're a keen adventure gamebook player, then you should try some of our exciting Combat Heroes gamebooks. They are available in bookshops or they can be ordered directly from us. Just complete the form below and enclose the right amount of money and the books will be sent to you at home.

Joe Dever
☐ WHITE WARLORD	£2.25
☐ BLACK BARON	£2.25
☐ EMERALD ENCHANTER	£2.50
☐ SCARLET SORCERER	£2.50

If you would like to order books, please send this form, and the money due to:
ARROW BOOKS, BOOKSERVICE BY POST, PO BOX 29, DOUGLAS, ISLE OF MAN, BRITISH ISLES. Please enclose a cheque or postal order made out to Arrow Books Ltd for the amount due including 15p per book for postage and packing both for orders within the UK and for overseas orders.

NAME...

ADDRESS...

....

Please print clearly.

THE LONE WOLF CLUB

The Lone Wolf Club offers you exciting opportunities to become further involved in Lone Wolf activities. Joe Dever writes the newsletter for the Club and there are competitions, events and the opportunity to collect Lone Wolf souvenirs and copies of the books signed by Joe.

If you are interested in becoming a member of the Lone Wolf Club, please write to The Lone Wolf Club, Beaver Books, 62–65 Chandos Place, London, WC2N 4NW, enclosing a large stamped addressed envelope or an international money order to cover postage if you live abroad or in Ireland.

RANDOM NUMBER TABLE

9	3	1	2	8	1	4	7	7	2
6	3	8	8	8	5	4	9	3	1
9	5	6	6	5	7	6	3	6	7
2	5	0	4	8	6	6	8	7	2
0	5	9	5	7	0	9	4	4	1
2	8	2	5	6	7	3	2	5	6
3	4	8	0	7	1	4	8	4	0
6	2	0	4	6	1	1	4	2	0
0	5	6	6	2	1	8	4	1	6
4	6	5	6	0	5	9	0	1	5